Mind Full of Scorpions

Copyright © 2006 Katherine Tapley-Milton
All rights reserved.
ISBN: 1-4196-4023-2

To order additional copies, please contact us.
BookSurge, LLC
www.booksurge.com
1-866-308-6235
orders@booksurge.com

KATHERINE
TAPLEY-MILTON

MIND FULL OF SCORPIONS

2006

Mind Full of Scorpions

TABLE OF CONTENTS

Introduction	xiii
The Tiger	1
Stories My Father Told Me As A Child	3
Wanting To Grow Up Dead	7
Heaven And Hell	9
They're Falling Like Flies	15
Getting Degrees, Dodging Hallucinations	19
Father, I've Died And Gone To Hell	27
The Fires Of The Mind	33
Moving Uptown	35
Why Do Some Psychiatrists Act Crazy?	37
Fitness Fiasco	41
The Day My Father Died	43
The Solitary Life	47
Miracles Occur In The Strangest Of Places	49
Epilogue : Bird On A Wire	51
Appendix: Songs, Articles, Poems, Sources Of Help	53
A. A Short Psychiatric History Lesson	55
B. The Thinkin' Song	57
C. Some Articles On Mental Illness	59
Famous Mentally Ill Persons	61
Famous Only In The Mind: An Insight Into Psychosis	67
Humor That Can Hurt Or Heal	69
TMS: An Alternative To Electroshock	73
Schizoaffective Disorder	75
What Is Missing In The System?	81
Is Reality Therapy In Reality?	85
What Is W.R.A.P.?	89
Should I Go See The Psychiatrist Well Dressed?	91

D. Poems On Experiencing Mental Illness	*95*
E. Sample Legal Forms	*111*
Power of Attorney for Personal Care	111
Advance Directive For Mental Health Treatment	113
Psychiatric Advance Directive Toolkit	123
F. Helpful Websites	*129*

FORWARD

Dear Readers:

Mind Full of Scorpions is a passionate account of the suffering someone can go through when living with a mental illness. And behind this terror and fear, we are awed at how those with such emotional challenges struggle to survive and often reclaim their lives by overcoming these overwhelming obstacles.

This life story authored by Katherine Tapley Milton is history in the making because it is the first one of its kind published by Our Voice / Notre Voix under *The Mary Huestis Pengilly Life Story / Activism Scholarship Writing Fund*. We hope to be able to publish many others in either official language in the years to come.

I would like to take this opportunity to thank and acknowledge New Brunswick's Assistant Deputy Minister for Mental Health, Ken Ross, for his ongoing support of this publication and having the foresight to see the strategic role Our Voice / Notre Voix can play in the landscape of mental health services in this province. On some levels, we are indeed blessed to have governmental leadership consistently supporting the consumer / survivor sector for over two decades! Many other jurisdictions in Canada envy New Brunswick's approach in this regard.

Please read Mind Full of Scorpions with an open mind so that your heart may be open to understanding.

Sincerely
Eugène LeBlanc
Publisher & Editor In Chief
Ourvoice-Notrevoix

INTRODUCTION

Where is she at, they wonder. Why does she behave that way? It's a long story and it hurts with the telling, but I need to tell it to someone, someone who will listen and pray...". –poem by Doug Burke

I want to take you on a journey to a strange world. It's a world perhaps that you have never thought about too much. No, this is not a story about how I was abducted by aliens or taken to outer space. This is a story about "inner space", a travel into the last frontier, the human mind. It is a horror story of sorts, not a syrupy sweet story about success and fame. I want to take you into a subject that society often finds taboo—the world of the mentally ill, deep inside a mind inhabited by scorpions.

"Why should I read such a book?" you might be asking. First, I would say that mental illness is no respecter of persons. Whether you are rich or poor, white or black, a VIP or an unknown, you can experience mental illness—one in four persons becomes mentally ill. Secondly, I believe that many people are still in the Dark Ages when it comes to dealing with the subject. There is a definite stigma surrounding it which causes much unnecessary suffering and loneliness for the individual affected. Thirdly, if you are admitted to a psychiatric hospital you will soon find out that there are many in the helping professions that should not be allowed around the emotionally ill because of their lack of compassion and an arrogant stance. The mental hospitals have rigid rules that try to fit the patient into a mold and "punish" him or her like a bad child. Patients are often not respected as persons of worth, but often plunged into shame and subhuman conditions, forced to live like prisoners of war instead of people that need to be cared, understood, and healed.

I have been a freelance writer for the last 30 years and I have done over 200 interviews of other people. In writing my own story I have done a lot of soul searching, because it is terrifying to face my inner pain. Some of my instincts tell me, "Let sleeping dogs lie" and not to make my personal pain public. However, I am like the Ancient Mariner that had an albatross around his neck; condemned to tell his tale. I will be forever haunted by the abuse I received in institutions and the stigma surrounding mental illness.

You may find that some of the scenes depicted in this book are disturbing, but I have tried to tell it like it is because I feel that society shouldn't continue to stick its head in the sand when it comes to mental illness. Come with me as I take you through my inner space odyssey as I show you my struggle with schizoaffective disorder.

***

Special Note: Some of the names have been altered to protect the anonymity of the persons involved.

THE TIGER

The Tyger

Tyger! Tyger! burning bright
In the forests of the night,
What immortal hand or eye
Could frame thy fearful symmetry?

In what distant deeps or skies
Burnt the fire of thine eyes?
On what wings dare he aspire?
What the hand dare seize the fire?

And what shoulder, and what art,
Could twist the sinews of thy heart?
And when thy heart began to beat,
What dread hand and what dread feet?

What the hammer, what the chain?
In what furnace was thy brain?
What the anvil? What dread grasp
Dare its deadly terrors clasp?...

—Excerpt from poem by William Blake (1794)

I will begin my story with life before mental illness plagued me when I was growing up in the country as a child. My home was a rather large reddish, shingled house on a hill in the place that my grandfather had, named "Frosty Hollow". When I was a child this seemed like a part of rural New Brunswick that was isolated from the rest of the world. Things moved slowly there. In the summer life consisted of berry picking, swimming in the pond, and drinking iced tea in the welcome coolness of a country kitchen. We picked Lady's Slippers and May flowers in the Spring, and in June the air would be filled with the sweet smell of new mown hay. I was close to my father and he showed me all the names of the mosses and plants in the woods. As a child I was taken to the local Anglican Church mainly because my mother and grandmother were of that faith and my pulpit-splitting great grandfather was an Anglican minister for over forty years.

My father was an agnostic and went to church to please my mother at Christmas and Easter. Since my father had the greatest influence over me I didn't relish going to church and would rather have been out riding my horse.

Father worked in one of the town's factories, "The Enterprise", where they made stoves and furnaces. My mother's relatives owned the place. There was a forty-year conflict between my father and my mother's relations. To me as a child the foundry was very frightening. I used to have to go inside to meet my father for a drive home from school. The megaton steel presses were slamming down to make metal stove parts and the forklifts were hectically tearing around corners. Hot molten lead looking like lava poured from the moulders' ladles as the men worked feverishly to make stove parts. The foundry was like a page out of a Charles Dickens novel, but it provided pay checks for half of the town's population. At noon and at five o'clock my father used to come home and rant and rave about the foundry. I watched as he turned bitter and angry. However, he was at his most relaxed when telling stories.

STORIES MY FATHER TOLD ME AS A CHILD

One of my father's quirks was to nick name people. Some of the characters in town were known as Soup Bone Joe, Bert Monkey, Tee-Hee, etc., (I have to admit that it is a trait that he passed on to me). After supper if he could find anyone at all to listen, my father used to trot out stories of Douglas Avenue and the old City of Saint John where he grew up. He also spun yarns about the local lore of Frosty Hollow where our old homestead was.

One of the Saint John stories that I like the best is about the Tapley's Saint Bernard dog. Around Christmas time the dog arrived home with a white package of sausages tied with a red ribbon. My grandmother called all the butcher shops and all her friends, but no one knew anything about the sausages. Each day the dog brought more and more of these packages, until Grandmother Tapley was frantic. My father and his brother, Uncle Charles, tracked the dog, but he led them on a wild goose chase. The questions that begs to be answered were "Where did the sausages come from and who was the person missing them?" I guess we will never know the answer.

Another story that my father told was of my rotund Grandfather Tapley who proudly brought a wool bathing suit home to my grandmother after a business trip to Boston. My grandmother, who loved to swim, sported the bathing suit while swimming in the Bay of Fundy and everything seemed to be going well. However, the bathing suit started shrinking and getting so tight that she called my father for a pair of scissors and a trench coat. Grandmother Tapley had to cut off the bathing suit and drape herself in the coat while she salvaged the last of her dignity.

Father frequently used to chuckle about the story of my grandmother Tapley and her special "tonic". Now you have to understand that she was a staunch, liquor-abstaining Baptist. She and her sisters took the tonic and said it helped them feel marvelous. However, scandal hit the Tapley family when it was discovered that the tonic was 90% Rye Whiskey!

Frosty Hollow had its own set of stories that my father told. One incident occurred when a neighbor who stuttered went to snare rabbits. When he went into our woods, he came back to our house, absolutely terrified and all he could get out was, "Now, John!" "Now John!" After he calmed himself a little he told of how a wild cat had jumped over his head while he was tending a snare.

In our house there were lots of Aunt Lilly and Uncle Jock stories. Jock had been gassed in WW I and a French doctor told him to be around coniferous trees for his health. With Grandfather Fisher's support he started the Frosty Hollow Inn. Apparently, when the Frosty Hollow Inn was purchased, old man Bulmer came with it. He was going senile and would occasionally urinate down the registers.

Aunt Lilly, who had been brought up in a hotel and took physical education, was expected to cook, but she didn't even know how to boil water. One incident my father told us about was that Aunt Lilly had tried to make bread that was totally inedible. Fearing Uncle Jock's wrath, and frequent swearing sessions she quickly threw the ruined bread at the head of Bulmer's Pond, which was right beside the Inn. When Uncle Jock came into the kitchen, the ducks swam by the window with the bread in their beaks, giving evidence of the culinary disaster. Uncle Jock was known as very high strung and wild.

Aunt Lilly was known in the family as the chocolate maker. Every special event was an occasion for Aunt Lilly to give her tasty home-made chocolates. However, strange things were found in them like pieces of glass, and dog hairs. One day I discovered why. If a chocolate fell on the floor Aunt Lilly simply picked it up and put it in the box.

Father also told about Uncle Rory, who had some flamboyant attacks of mental illness. On one occasion he worked on a luxury liner as the ship's doctor. In the evening when the passengers were dressed in tuxedos and ballroom gowns, Rory strode in totally naked.

Another Uncle Rory story was about his visit to the States. He had six children and one of them got scratched up when he fell into the tiger's cage. Rory was ready to sue the whole U.S. government. He often wrote to letters to Eleanor Roosevelt, although no one knows for sure if she ever wrote him back.

Although mentally ill, Uncle Rory became a physician and graduated with the highest average ever seen at McMaster University. He rewrote the ten commandments and designed a coordinated welfare state complete with holistic healing concepts. In 1945, Rory was admitted to a mental hospital called Centracare in Saint John, and almost had a frontal lobotomy, but his wife wouldn't let the doctors do it. I met him when he was in his seventies and suffering severely from Parkinson's disease. In his writings, Uncle Rory referred to himself as a "hectic character".

I guess that through my mother's gene pool I must have inherited Uncle Rory's madness. For some inexplicable reason I never felt I fully fit in anywhere and my shyness was extreme. When I was invited to childhood birthday parties I cried because I was scared to go. Field days at school were disastrous for me because I was about as athletic as a platypus. Nobody wanted me on their team and I was left in the dust at the track. To ease the pain of my social isolation I began painting and drawing. My favorite subject was the tiger. To me a tiger with its fierceness represented the unnamed fears lurking in my young mind, fears that I could not express. Little did I know that my fairly secure world would end up being torn asunder and plunged into a nightmare of pain with a mind full of scorpions.

WANTING TO GROW UP DEAD

"Why is light given to those in misery, and life to the bitter of soul, to those who long for death that does not come, who search for it more than for hidden treasure ..." (Job 3:20-21 NIV)

When I was a child I was frequently referred to as an "afterthought" and mistaken for my sister. I didn't look like her, but people didn't seem to realize that I was born eleven years after she was. My two brothers, were older still and they were off and married by the time I was six years old.

I'd say that my mental illness started when I was about fourteen. Practically, everyone who I went to high school with said I was either crazy or on street drugs. I hid under tables, laughed uncontrollably, had periods of deep depression, and jumped out of my skin when anyone came up behind me. In grade eight I had been on the Student Council and had a few friends, but by grade nine, I constantly thought of suicide, became morose and depressed. Other kids wanted to be doctors or lawyers, but all I wanted was to grow up dead. Paranoia stalked me constantly. I had a feeling of being pursued by an invisible enemy. Going around corners, up stairs, or venturing into a darkened room heightened these feelings. Then came the hallucinations and voices and I was plunged into a private hell that nobody understood. I tried to read psychology books to figure out what was happening to me and I dabbled in a new religion every week. But, I concluded that life was meaningless and as the existentialists like Jean Paul Sartre and Albert Camu would say, "absurd" or a "bad joke". The more I read the more confused I got. As I listened to my favorite record, Simon and Garfunkel's "Sounds of Silence" my mind was drugged into a deep depression by the words, "... I am a rock, I am an island ... hiding in my room, safe within my womb, I touch no one and no one touches me...". I felt like a modern day leper, the mental illness putting me beyond the pale of civilization.

Eventually, my depression led me to take 300 pills out of the medicine cabinet—everything from Aspirin to tranquilizers—and I swallowed them all painfully burning my esophagus in the process. I took the overdose at 9 pm and by 1 am I told my parents what I had done. What saved me was that I had had a vision of there being no one there to ride my chestnut horse, Golden Glow, and it made me incredibly sad because I wanted to ride her again. My parents were disbelieving that I swallowed so many pills, but they took salt and water and poured it down my throat to make me vomit. It was the same thing that they did to the dog when it swallowed rat poison. I was never seen by a doctor or taken to a hospital. My hands got black and puffed up and I was sweating profusely. But I lived on. Other suicide attempts followed. One day I stole a pistol from my father's gun room and sat on a stump in the woods for three hours, trying to get the nerve up to pull the trigger. Another time I had swallowed a bunch of aspirins and then tried to drink powered mustard and water to purge my body. While other teenagers were thinking of going to the prom, I was plotting my demise.

HEAVEN AND HELL

At the age of sixteen I was invited to a Billy Graham crusade in my own hometown. There was a film titled, "The Lost Generation" and I went to see it protesting and mocking all things Christian. An evangelist stood at the front of Convocation Hall and gave the alter call. No one went up to talk to him. However, I was so angry that I wanted to argue with him and tell him that there was no such thing as truth. I disputed with him for three hours and finally he said that he would like to pray with me. He gave me the sinner's prayer and the next thing that I knew I was down on my knees praying it. I read it as fast as I could and he told me that I now had Jesus in my heart. For some bizarre reason I thought that Jesus was not portable and I wanted to remain in the hall because I thought that I would lose Him. They finally convinced me to leave, assuring me that the Holy Spirit did travel inside of me. For the next year I was on a spiritual high, though the mood swings continued to haunt me. I joined Inter Varsity Christian Fellowship even before I went to University and always asked a lot of theological questions. Most people are saved by the fear of hell, but I was saved by the love of God. I didn't believe in hell and the devil until about nine months after I was saved, simply because I didn't know it was part of the Christian faith. I made lots of mistakes as a new Christian, buttonholing people and preaching to them; generally making myself obnoxious. It was at this time I started going to the Baptist Church and got a solid grounding in doctrine.

By the age of eighteen I enrolled in The Atlantic Baptist Bible College where I took my fist year of university. I was seeing a psychiatrist and he was a choleric man, who generally made me worse by the sarcastic comments he made. My illness was blamed on a bad adolescence and I was given Librium and Valium which were very addictive. I was still a victim of frequent visual hallucinations, voices in my head, and paranoia. In the 1970's one did not dare reveal that one was seeing a psychiatrist. It would have been a scandal.

That same year I got a job at Centracare in Saint John. It was formerly called the "Lancaster Lunatic Asylum" and was an ancient brick building next to the Reversing Falls. I was lying in bed, very sick with bronchitis, but I begged my parents to take me to Saint John so I could work as a psychiatric ward attendant for the summer. I found an apartment with some Christian girls and began work. When I had a tour of Centracare I felt that a horror movie should have been filmed there. The old elevators creaked and groaned and on every ward you could hear terrible moaning and crying. There was a ward downstairs that had profoundly mentally challenged children who ate their own excrement and had to wear hockey helmets to protect their heads. For a naive eighteen year old country girl it was a rude awakening.

Although I had not dated much when I was in high school, suddenly men started finding me very attractive. A Native Canadian ward attendant started making comments about how pretty I was and other men seemed interested as well. One long weekend, when the other girls were out of the apartment I was very upset and was crying hysterically. I suddenly remembered that my school guidance counselor had given me a phone number. He had said, "If you get into trouble or just need to talk, give this guy a call." So I called.

The man on the phone said that he would pick me up in his car and take me to his office which was in city hall on King Street. He worked for the Department of Youth. He was a tall man with a beard and I went with him, not knowing who else to turn to. In his office he talked to me as a counselor would to a client for about the next ten minutes. Then he started making comments about my breasts. He told me, "I can't do therapy with you unless you go to bed with me. I can tell so much more about you if we sleep together." I thought that maybe this was some new form of therapy, but I told him that I was a Christian and that I wouldn't do anything like that.

However, I desperately wanted someone to talk to. I was frightened, hallucinating, and in a city where I didn't know anybody. My mind kept breaking down into psychosis. Many times I kept banging my head against the wall to try to stop the visual hallucinations, but they kept going on and I lived in constant torment.

One day walking back from the bus stop, I was chased by a man in a car in broad daylight and I started running. The man trapped me at the corner and asked if I would go to bed with him. Even though I was panic stricken I shouted, "Go to hell!" That Night as I slept at night the building on the other side of the street burned down and this really upset me because my biggest fear is fire. I was about as upset as a person could get, but I still had the therapist's phone number. Finally, when the others were out of the apartment, I cried into the phone, "I need you to come over!" I had made the decision to sacrifice my virginity, because I didn't care anymore. Anything that would possibly relieve the emotional pain and the nightmare I would do.

The therapist came over to the apartment and we ended up in the bedroom. I had never seen a man undressed before and I guess there was the element of curiosity there. I was away from my parents for the first time in my life and there was no one watching over me. When I was in the bed I curled up in a fetal position. I was scared to death and felt only numbness. From that night on there were many sessions of me going to his office and having him sexually fondle me. He called me his "sex kitten", and I submitted numbly just to get someone to talk to. He told me he had a wife and new baby at home. Little did I know that this guy was having sex with small children and I was not the only eighteen year old who had been molested by him. I heard that today he is doing over twenty years in an Ontario prison, because fifteen different women came forward to accuse him in court. I was not one of those women, since I knew nothing about the proceedings. He was a man who felt he could sin with impunity and justified his actions by saying that he was good at sex and female clients were led to believe that it was all part of the "therapy".

Also, that summer, I started seeing a social worker at the mental health clinic near the apartment. There was a long set of stairs leading up to his office. One day I was going up to see him and the secretary spoke to me telling me that he already had a client. I had had my back turned to her and my nerves were so bad that I jumped up half a flight of stair and landed on the window ledge. I stayed there curled up and totally paranoid. The only psychiatric drug that I knew the name of was Stelazine. I asked for some, because a girl I knew at the Atlantic Baptist College had been on it. I didn't know what it did, other than it was a tranquilizer. The psychiatrist handed me a big box of samples. I started taking it, not having been told any of the side effects. Soon my eyes started rolling up inside their sockets and I started shaking violently. A male coworker who was a in the apartment at the time thought that I was taking an epileptic seizure, since he was epileptic himself. The physical discomfort was unbearable, so I went to the hospital, which was nearby. They just put a warm sheet over me and let me lie in a bed for awhile, then sent me home. I didn't know that it was the Stelazine that was causing my symptoms and I had never heard of the side effect drug, Cogentin. The girls in the apartment started turning against me. They thought that I was stoned on street drugs, which of course was disgraceful for a Christian.

I quit working at Centracare after a month, because I couldn't take it anymore. You never knew when a patient might assault you and I was given a homicidal patient to baby-sit. The staff warned me that certain colors would make one particular patient very violent. There was one patient that went insane because of untreated syphilis, others had organic brain syndrome due to alcohol abuse, still others had schizophrenia or manic depressive illness or were mentally challenged. My idealistic dreams of helping the mentally ill went up in smoke as I left Centracare.

Staying in Saint John, I enrolled in college courses of Personality Theory and Political Science. While the professor was talking about politics I was seated like all the other students, taking notes. A really bad hallucination hit me. A wart on my hand seemed to grow in size. It engulfed my hand, then my arm and body. I wanted to scream and scream from the sheer terror of it, yet I kept taking notes and no one caught on to the turmoil and panic that I was feeling. Back in my bedroom I smashed my head against the wall, trying to make the hallucinations stop. During this period in Saint John I started seeing the ward clerk and on impulse I agreed to marry him. We went to see the chaplain and apparently he alerted my parents. My father threatened my boyfriend that if he didn't leave me alone he would lose his job, but I was left unaware of all this.

Once home again in Sackville, I made plans to go to Ontario to live with my brother. In the back of my mind was that maybe they had better mental health care there. My psychosis continued to be a problem. One day in my brother's house I plugged the vacuum in the kitchen and the plug exploded. The rest of the day I spent huddled by the couch, hallucinating and paranoid. I couldn't sleep and my anxiety was exploding. I begged my brother to take me to the Royal Ottawa Hospital. Finally, he did.

THEY'RE FALLING LIKE FLIES

The blunting of conscious motivation, and the ability to solve problems under the influence of Chlorpromazine ... resemble nothing so much as the effects of frontal lobotomy. The lobotomy syndrome was familiar top psychiatrists in 1954 (the year that Chlorpromazine was introduced into North America) because so many lobotomized patients had accumulated in mental hospitals. Research has suggested that lobotomies and chemicals like Chlorpromazine may cause their effects in the same way, by disrupting the activity of the neuro-chemical, dopamine. At any rate, a psychiatrist would be hard-put to distinguish a lobotomized patient from one treated with Chlorpromazine."

(Found in Dr. Caligari's Psychiatric Drugs published by the Network Against Psychiatric Assault, Berkley, California, 1994, written by Peter Sterling, PhD.)

The Royal Ottawa Hospital was the first mental institution that I had ever entered as a patient. The first thing that I noticed was that the patients seemed to be falling down on the floor and having to have the staff pick them up and put them in a bed or a chair. I was both curious and frightened. What kind of ailment would make people fall like flies? I didn't know how one should comport oneself as a mental hospital patient, so I acted strangely, because I was supposed to be crazy wasn't I? I stalked down the ward with extra long strides. What would they say about me? Would they kick me out because I wasn't crazy enough? I certainly didn't want that to happen. I wanted therapy. I wanted them to stop the hallucinations, the insomnia, the interminable terror.

I was put in a ward with other patients and had to stand in a long line to get medication. I didn't know the names of hardly any psychiatric medications, but I soon learned the name Chlorpromazine. It dried my mouth out so that my tongue stuck to the roof of my mouth, my lips cracked, and I would be in the middle of a sentence and forget my thoughts. I felt mentally handicapped. A nice lady psychologist tested my I.Q., but I know that I must have scored very low on the test results. In any case she guessed that I was in the superior range of intelligence, at least that's what she told me.

One night I was feeling self-destructive. Here I was at nineteen years old locked up in a mental institution when I should be studying for a career in college. I had been working on making paper flowers and had some thick wire on my dresser. I took the wire and tried to make cuts in my wrists. One of the male nurses saw me and immediately jumped on top of me, pinning me down on the bed. The shock of a male body on me reminded me of the abuse from the therapist in Saint John. I panicked, because he wouldn't move off me. So, to free myself I bit into his arm as hard as I could. He jumped off me and my punishment came swiftly. It was what I call "The Cup of Hemlock", a whole medicine cup full of Chlorpromazine was forced down my throat. When it took effect I thought that I was dying. I could hardly breathe or move and it felt like there was a heavy weight on my chest. A lady came to visit me the next day from the church and I could not even roll an eyeball to acknowledge her. I felt like I had been buried alive. I would much rather have had a cloth straight jacket rather than that chemical one.

From time to time I had seen a rather friendly, jolly psychiatrist on the wards and he impressed me. Dr. D. was from Peru and very approachable. One day I begged him to help me he gave me a hug in a room off of the ward. From that day on I became his patient. He took me off the Chlorpromazine and put me on some very mild medication. He liked to hug me and I became sexually attracted to him. My fantasies were filled with him. He told me I was like a fish out of water in the city, and he was right—I was really a country girl at heart.

I was so stressed adjusting to Ottawa, the hospital, and my illness that at that period of my life I walked all twisted with one shoulder higher than the other. The depression and confusion got so bad that I would walk out into the middle of Carling Avenue by the hospital regardless of how much traffic was going by. It was a very busy thoroughfare and the cars used to honk at me, but I was too much in a daze to realize that I was in the middle of danger. God must have wanted me to live, because it was a miracle that I didn't get run over.

One day a social worker came and met with me and told me that I would soon be released and if I agreed, I could be sent to a half-way house on Maclaren Avenue. It was composed of five Catholic nuns and five individuals with serious problems. When I got there I was placed in a bedroom with one other nun. There was another woman from the hospital whom I didn't know, a pregnant teenager, and people with various bad situations. I insisted on attending Algonquin College, despite professional advice not to, and took Developmental Psychology and Social Psychology. I had to get up at 6 am when it was still cold and dark and catch a series of buses to get to the college. One day I jumped on the wrong bus and went way out of Ottawa. I called my sister-in-law crying and she said, "Where are you?" "I don't know!" I wailed. However, she told me to get the bus on the opposite side of the road and it should get me back to Ottawa.

Due to a learning disability I've always had a lousy sense of direction. One day I went out exploring the neighbourhood and passed a shop where there was an enormous set of steer horns—long ones like my father had always wanted. They were only $19.95 so I wrote a cheque and bought them. The clerk wrapped the middle in newspaper, but when I carried them the horns protruded a lot. It didn't take a long time to realize that I was terribly lost. As I walked on the sidewalk a truck nearly crashed as the driver gawked at the horns. I kept trudging and trudging until I could see something that looked familiar. Finally I found the half-way house and that Christmas I proudly took the horns home to present to my father.

While living with the nuns I used to go to the Rideau Canal and skate. Since I wasn't sleeping at all I got into a manic state and in the daytime skated ten miles at top speed. When I was in the corridor of the college one day my black pants started to fall off of me. I had lost weight so rapidly that I hadn't realized it. It was quite a predicament to have to hold my pants up and hold all my text books too while waiting for the bus.

After a year in Ottawa I went back home to Sackville and though I was still in a bad state I decided I would try to please my family by enrolling in a registered nursing assistant program at the Community College. I moved into the nurses' residence and studied hard. But however hard I tried I could never make a bed up to the instructors' standards and when I was doing the practical work I left a bed rail down and tried to feed a senile old lady breakfast without putting her dentures in. The old lady was happily eating her porridge, but it didn't impress my supervisor. After six months I was called to the head nurse's office and told to leave the program. I heard later that I had gotten the highest mark of all the exams in the nursing school. I was great in theory, but terrible in practice. My father came to collect me and my stuff and we drove home in his yellow Volkswagen Rabbit. On the way back to Sackville smoke started billowing out from the engine. We stopped and a couple of men got some water from the swamp to try to cool the engine down. I thought that the car was going to explode, but it didn't.

GETTING DEGREES, DODGING HALLUCINATIONS

When I was twenty-one, my mother badgered me into getting a drivers license. She kept saying "What if somebody was sick and you couldn't drive them to the hospital?" I was so nervous that I didn't want to drive when I was sixteen. My parents took me on the old dirt roads where very few vehicles traveled, so I couldn't do much damage. I practiced parallel parking next to my father's International Scout and dinged the tailgate slightly. Eventually it came time for the test and I had a grumpy, sour-faced man that whistled all the time I was driving. I passed the first time and therefore I could travel the three miles to town where the university was.

I had done ten university credits at various other universities, but I went to Mount Allison University for the final two years of my B.A. I was a serious, diligent student. Since I had to have one science credit to graduate I picked a Fortran computer course, which was probably the last thing I should have chosen. I had failed algebra in grade eleven and Fortran was based on that. The pressure of the course made me hallucinate and get very ill. There wasn't any computer at Mount A in those days and we had to take cards, punch things into them and send them to Fredericton.

One day I picked up a card that must have had holes already punched in it and I did my assignment and thought all was well. However, the next day the director called me on the carpet because all the students programs had garbage written all over them and were ruined. Since the professors took off marks for every day that the assignments were late I was in disgrace.

By that time, I was a nervous wreck at university I was put on a low dose of Stalinize again by a family doctor. It made me feel like I was mentally challenged. I couldn't remember back to a time where my mind had worked. When I went into my history professor's office I confessed, "I think that there has been a mistake. I'm at university, but I'm stupid. He talked to me, encouraged me, and said that he would help me get off of the pills. He advised that I get some supplements at the health food store like brewers yeast and desiccated liver tablets. These did give me amazing energy.

While I was trying to get off the drugs I didn't sleep at night and my brain felt like there was a cattle prod searing it with electric shocks every five minutes. After I succeeded at getting off the Stelazine I felt better. My intelligence seemed to come back. I would study until two in the morning and get up at six, since I was behind in my work. When I graduated with a B.A. it was a perfect sunny day, the swans were swimming serenely in the Mt. A pond and I was elated. I felt that I had conquered mental Illness and that my future looked bright.

I debated over what master's degree I would take. Would it be social work at Dalhousie University or would it be somewhere else? Finally, I decided to go to Ontario Theological Seminary in Willowdale, near Toronto, because I felt that I wanted to help people spiritually. I envisioned being a missionary or Bible teacher and I was willing to go overseas if God called me there.

While in a French immersion course at the Universite de Moncton, I met a journalist who wanted someone to share the driving to Toronto and give her fifteen dollars for the gas, since she had a small car. The opportunity seemed an answer to prayer, so I packed up and went with her. It was in September that we started out and the scenery was breathtaking. The Appalachian Mountains in Quebec and the Sumac trees around Tweedsville, Ontario were wonderful. The driving went alright except when I turned onto the 401 highway, near Toronto. Coming from a small town that only had one traffic light I had never seen so many lanes and was overwhelmed. I almost hit an older model car which had black fins.

MIND FULL OF SCORPIONS

At that point I quickly pulled over to the side of the road and told the woman who owned the car to take over.

By the time I got to the seminary I was completely stressed out. I didn't know what to do in the subway to get tokens and I was terrified of getting caught in one of the subway doors. People were rude and impatient and nearly stomped on my head as I bent over to pick up a token I had dropped. I was suffering from culture shock and when I closed my eyes the pavement with its white line kept hitting me in the face while I kept seeing the black fin of the car that I almost hit. Within twenty-four hours of being in seminary I went psychotic. I knew that I need help so I contacted the school's psychologist and when he first saw me he said, "You want to jump out of that window, don't you?" Surprised that it was that obvious, I hesitated, pinned in fear. Finally I said, "Yes, I do".

I had come to seminary only wanting to do God's will. I was praying, memorizing Scripture, and reading the Bible, but the monitor's were told to keep an eye on me because I was hallucinating and suicidal. Where had I gone wrong? Why hadn't all this prayer helped me stay sane?

Somehow through the madness I still had a drive to succeed academically and I was known by my professors as a good student. I studied as hard as I could, but there were days when I was too ill to work. I abused myself by staying up all night and drinking coffee, then rolling into an eight o'clock class. That first year at seminary I was totally manic. I ran seven miles a day and squirmed constantly in the chair as I sat talking to the counsellor. Although single and celebrate I was tortured by sexual desires almost bordering on nymphomania. Sometimes the visual hallucinations were so bad that I put my hands over my eyes and backed myself into a corner, trying to will them to stop. My hallucinations at that time were a kaleidoscopic blend of horrors. For instance, I saw skulls, bones, parts of soldiers' bodies and things I can't verbally describe. However, the net effect was terror and deep emotional pain. I also suffered from feelings that people were out to get me and had interminable insomnia. At that time I refused medication on the grounds that it would affect my ability to study. However, I became a problem to the institution.

Rod, the psychologist, insisted that I go down to the North York Hospital to be admitted. He and a school monitor accompanied me. First an intern came in and asked me questions like, "Do you get messages from your television set?" and "Do you talk to God?" I replied that, "No, I don't get messages from T.V. "and "Yes, of course I talk to God, as I am a Christian and studying in a seminary." The intern wrote my answers down and then went to get the head of psychiatry to ask me all the same questions over again. I desperately didn't want a hospital stay, so I persuaded them that I would see a psychiatrist and take medication. The psychiatrist strongly recommended a stay in the hospital, but being in a manic state made me quite convincing.

I don't exactly know how I managed to get through my master's degree, except for the fact that I was absolutely determined to do well academically and I had Rod supporting me. Anger was a factor as well, since a family doctor in Moncton, New Brunswick told me that I was a hopeless schizophrenic, would never get even a B. A., and spend the rest of my life in a convent. The prediction that I would never amount to anything haunted me and the need to prove the doctor wrong compelled me to keep studying and hanging on.

The second year of my master's degree was equally frightening. From mania I slipped into a state of total numbness and burn out. When I stepped into a hot bath I could hardly feel the heat. I felt that everything and everybody was distant and that I was in limbo. One night I plugged the Vicks vaporizer into a razor outlet in the room and machine started burning and the plug exploded. One of the girls quickly thought to turn the power off, because the plug could not be pulled out of the outlet on the wall. I got so emotionally numb and depressed that I got to the point where I didn't even care about my degree. I just wanted to forget getting the last half credit that I needed to graduate and go back home to the Maritimes. Rod refused to let me do that, so the dean gave me special permission to do a mini thesis when I went back home to Sackville. He got me to pick from a variety of thesis topics and I chose the federal headship of Adam, one of the most difficult subjects in theology.

I worked hard on the paper for months, and mailed the thesis to the seminary. I got an A + on it, so my degree was completed and I graduated in May, 1981. My parents weren't going to go to my graduation, but I shamed them in to it. It was a beautiful ceremony with all of us in our black gowns and mortarboard hats, and as I stepped on the stage I was proud of my effort. For me, getting my masters degree was like Terry Fox running with only one leg across Canada. However, I don't have a single photograph of my triumph, as my family forgot to bring the camera.

Even though I got the Master of Theological Studies degree my vision of becoming an overseas missionary was crushed. After the first year of my masters I went on a summertime short term mission in Ireland. One of the reasons I chose the Emerald Isle was because it was dangerous. There was a lot of bombing in Belfast and I hoped that I would die there, allegedly a martyr. Going to Ireland, my motivation was a mixture of wanting to evangelize and desiring death. Ireland is a beautiful country sort of like Prince Edward Island in some ways and I was there six and one half weeks. We had a drama team and I played one of the "seeds" in the Biblical Parable of the Seeds. I jumped up and down, which was supposed to represent the seed trying to get through the soil. The head missionary wakened us at five forty-five each morning, bellowing, "Get up! Do you want to sleep your whole life away?" I was not getting adequate sleep and was severely stressed. There came a point when I got totally paranoid and thought that the whole mission team was plotting against me. Mary, one woman who was a nurse, befriended me and looked after me like she was a hen and I was her chick. However, every day I had to go with a minister and walk from house to house and present the gospel. One night we rode to Belfast in an aging Volkswagen van and sang in a church. Afterwards, the people, eager for fellowship, kept us up until 2 o'clock in the morning. As we traveled in the dark through Belfast we could see the bombed out buildings and wreckage. When I came back home after the Ireland episode I realized that my mental illness wouldn't allow me to be a missionary, I was too fragile to get knocked around overseas.

After seminary I cast around for a job and went for an interview at a nursing home in Nova Scotia. While I was being interviewed a nurse came to the door and said that my parents had been involved in a car crash. I thought that this was impossible, since they were parked by the nursing home, waiting for me. The boss offered to take me to the hospital. My father was in intensive care because of his heart and my mother had a big cut on her head. In the end I did get the job, but really I was too sick to work and it ended badly. I worked there for about a year as an activity director, but I was scared of the boss and I wouldn't pick up my pay check without being told because I thought that there would be a pink slip in it.

One day, the boss mentioned to me that I would look better if I lost weight. I rashly went on liquid, herbal diet to get the weight off that the psychiatric medications had put on. When she told me to take the company van and go do an errand down town, I meekly obeyed. The psychiatrist I was seeing had me on massive amounts of medication, plus I wasn't eating, so I was stoned and didn't realize it. In the end, I backed the van out of the driveway and across the road into a parked car with two people in the back of it. Fortunately no one was hurt, but the car and van were damaged. At that point the boss fired me on the spot.

I felt like it was the end of my world. I attended a day hospital for a while, at the suggestion of my psychiatrist, but the staff seemed to criticize me rather than build me up and I seemed to be getting worse. For years I had volunteered at the minimum security prison where I played my guitar and talked to the inmates. One weekend I went to an encounter group sponsored by the chaplain. I don't remember much of it, except that about fifty prisoners and some volunteers sat around in a group at the chapel and talked. Someone told me years later that I had been viciously criticized by a certain individual and that that put me over the edge.

Meanwhile, the psychiatrist kept giving me more and more Elavil, plus mega doses of Trilafon, Ativan, and Xanax. He kept saying, "I don't know how much medication you need." and would prescribe more each time I called him. At that time, I had been going to the Diet Centre and had lost a lot of weight, eventually getting down to 108 pounds. With all the dieting and overdosing of medication my mind snapped when the psychiatrist said, "You depend too much on your mother." At the day hospital kitchen I blurted out, "I want to kill him!" to another patient. My height is only five feet tall and the doctor was a chunky six foot four, so I couldn't have done much damage. However, I blame the over medication and his constant criticism on why I turned on him. He used to tell me that one of the nurses reported to him that I was seen at a movie theatre chewing gum like a cow, and he criticized me because he said I walked hunched over like an old woman.

At the day hospital I stole a knife from the kitchen and tried to cut myself behind a door. I called a friend who was a teacher and she came and picked me up. She recalls that everyone was hiding from me and that I must have been in a manic state because I was eating carrots and spitting the butts out of the car window as fast as I could. Since she couldn't stay with me because she had to teach, she left me at my family doctor's office. I walked out of the waiting room and cut my arms up with a razor. In a daze I walked around town. I went to the health food store and up to the history department, shocking everyone I met, and not knowing it.

FATHER, I'VE DIED AND GONE TO HELL

In the earlier days of the Hospital, even down to quite recent times, the mode of commitment of the insane was such an easy and free from formality that a few words hastily scribbled upon a chance scrap of paper were sufficient to place a supposed insane patient in the Hospital and deprive him of his personal liberty. If he did not remain passive, chains or some other form of mechanical restraint were used. Once in the cells, or quarters for insane, the patient had no appeal from the opinion of the attending physician

Once confined, the very confinement is admitted as the strongest of all proofs that a man must be mad. When, after suffering so much wrong, he has an opportunity of speaking to the appointed visitors of the house,—supposing him to be confined where he can be visited, and supposing him not to give way to his feelings, but to control them,—his entreaties, his anxious representations, his prayers for liberty, what do they avail!"

(Written by John Conolly
(1794-1866) a distinguished professor of medicine in the University of London and superintendent of the Middlesex County LunaticAsylum). Found in <u>The Age of Madness</u> by Thomas Szaz.

My second hospital experience was to be the worst of all. As my parents drove me up to the aging white and red brick building situated by the Reversing Falls, I knew that I was at the mercy of whoever had the keys to the locked door. When I was a child and used to visit my aunt in Saint John I think I remember seeing large iron cages sitting on the lawn at what was called Centracare. There were spooky stories that divers found skeletons of patients with chains around them at the bottom of the Reversing Falls. When I was eighteen, there was a month when I had worked at Centracare as a psychiatric ward attendant, and I had all the keys to the wards. I knew that the inside of the institution would have been a good place to film a Stephen King movie. There were creaking, ancient elevators, winding basement corridors, iron barred windows, and always the din of people moaning and crying. In the very bottom of the institution it was said there were actual dungeons. It used to be called The Lancaster Lunatic Asylum. I remember when I was a prison volunteer that an inmate told me that he spent time on the forensic unit and he exclaimed, "I was damn glad to get back to jail!" My experience as a ward attendant did not prepare me for what I was to endure as an inmate of Centracare. After being admitted, I spent a sleepless night in a small room with two beds. One bed was occupied by a manic depressive patient who talked and giggled constantly until the sleeping pills knocked her out at night. I was exhausted, but a hard-boiled nurse got me up early for breakfast which consisted of rubberized toast. The food had lain inside the metal tops that covered the trays, and it reminded me of cartoons I had seen where someone had tried to eat a rubber chicken and it snapped back in his face. As I picked at cold lifeless eggs, a small woman named Jenny vomited up her breakfast, while the staff yelled at her. Willie, and old man with Alzheimer's disease stood up and urinated on the floor. Darrel, a young paraplegic was fighting with the orderly who was trying to get him to eat, while Gertie, an obese geriatric patient kept up a constant moaning noise. In the background was the swearing of the staff and the loud clanging of meal trays. They never gave you time to eat. You had to gulp down what you could really fast.

Soon, I was told that the psychologist wanted me in his office for some testing. He literally shook me to wake me up. I tried to answer his questions, but I fell back asleep again. I told him that I was too drugged to continue, but he insisted that I do the tests saying that the drugs made no difference to the outcome. Days and days of testing went on. I was supposed to put wooden puzzles together, remember flash cards, and retell stories while being completely stoned and only half conscious from all the heavy drugging. In the end the psychologist told the psychiatrist that he suspected I had brain damage. They sent me off to the Regional Hospital for a CAT scan on my head to see if I was brain-damaged.

My psychiatrist was a black man whose accent was hard to understand. He treated me like I was a bad child. When he was going away for a couple of days he overdosed me with 30 milligrams of Haldol, to "keep me out of trouble". You had to stand in line for your pills and I had no option but to take the medication or else the staff would have gotten nasty and forced me. You didn't want to buck the hospital staff or you would end up being pinned down with a needle in your butt.

I heard that political prisoners from Russia complained to the Western media that they were tortured with a horrible drug. That drug was Haldol. Since I was given so much Haldol I went into an oculorgyric crisis, which is what happens when the medication causes your eyeballs to roll back in your head and stick there. It is excruciatingly uncomfortable and terrifying. When this started to happen to me I went to the nurse's station and begged for the antidote—the side effect pill Cogentin. She rudely informed me "You'll have to get a lost worse before we'll do anything about it." My neck arched back and my eyeballs were stuck staring up at a light bulb. I was in physical agony and could not believe the cruelty of someone who would leave me like that. This bad reaction to the medication went on for days and days.

The pay phone was my only contact with the outside world, but the competition for its use was fierce among the patients and it was difficult to hear over the din of the ward. I remember calling my parents long distance and begging them to get me out of Centracare, but I was certified which meant that legally I couldn't leave. Sobbing into the phone I told my father, "I must have died and gone to hell."

Things on the ward seemed to get rougher and you were always scared of getting a punch in the head. A mentally handicapped teenage boy hit an old lady with his fist one day and I was always terrified of a three hundred pound woman who was ranting and raving and always being dragged off to seclusion. Gertie's moaning kept up all night without any breaks at all. An old skinny patient that had a bad rash was always getting into my bed under the sheets. Every time she did that, and it was always several times a day I had to strip the bed and make it over again. When I tried to take a bath they had the water fixed so that it was never hot, it only got lukewarm. I was in there bathing one night and a senile old man wandered in while I was naked in the bath tub. Both men and women were kept on the same ward with no partitions.

My only solace was reading and playing guitar. Someone had loaned me a book I was very interested in, but the staff would not let me sit in my room quietly and read it. I was forced to stay outside on the word were it was impossible to concentrate because of the danger and the noise. When my roommate went home I was the only one in my room, so I hoped that I could keep the light on and read all night. I never slept anyway, so why not read instead of just lying there tortured by my disturbed thoughts and boredom. I got away with it for a few nights, but the staff discovered me and forbid me to have the light on past 10 pm.

Nights were always filled with continual conflict with the attendants that carried the flashlights and checked in your room every hour, shining the light in your eyes. Being hyper and unable to sleep made me hate staying in bed. However, in the institution the cardinal rule is if it's officially bedtime you have to be lying on your bed. The psychologist made a behaviour modification plan for my insomnia. He told me that if I was not sleeping I should get out of bed so that I would not associate my bed with insomnia. Of course the night staff would not believe what I said and herded me to bed anyway.

One Sunday morning my friends were allowed to take me out for part of the day. It was like I was being let out of prison. They took me to a restaurant here the food was very greasy and then we had a bumpy ride to their camp. I did not enjoy the trip, because

I felt suddenly nauseous. When I got back to Centracare, I did nothing but vomit for the next three months. I could not even keep water down. Shots of Gravol were useless. To make matters worse, the windows were always open and the rotten egg smell from the pulp mill nearby was always pouring in like a thick yellow, noxious fog. As the weeks turned into months I became weaker and couldn't dress myself. My roommate walked by me on the bed and announced, "You're going to die, I know it!" However, the psychiatrist and staff blamed me for making myself sick. I knew they were wrong, but they almost had me convinced that I was so crazy that I couldn't even perform a natural function like eating.

It really did feel like I was going to die. I did not have the strength to sit up in a chair anymore, but the staff would not allow me to lie on my bed in the daytime. They would yell at me when I slumped over the chair due to my physical weakness and they tried to force me to sit up straight, which was impossible. Just as I had given up hope of recovering, the psychiatrist called me to his office off the ward. Somehow I summoned the last bit of strength I possessed and made it to see him. He told me that he had been reading that if the antidepressant Elavil is withdrawn too quickly it could cause the vomiting and shaking and weakness that I was experiencing. Before I was admitted to Centracare I was on massive amounts of drugs and on 350mgs of Elavil. The psychiatrist had taken all of the old medication away without tapering it off. He had almost killed me and there was no apology.

After months of the hopeless atmosphere of Centracare, I was a broken woman. When I was allowed out for a walk on the grounds I looked across the lawn to the white water cascading below in the Reversing Falls. It was swirling down in eddying pools and it mesmerized me. There wasn't a fence or barrier of any kind between myself and the Falls. I wanted to jump over and I knew that many Centracare patients before me had jumped. I was almost off the grounds when my roommate yelled at me, "I heard that you are getting out today, congratulations!" At first I couldn't believe it, but yes it was true. I was being released from the jaws of hell.

KATHERINE TAPLEY-MILTON

After I got out of Centracare I was bitter and angry. I was furious at God for all the suffering I had experienced and I doubted that He loved me. I was sent to a psychologist who saw me every week and he showed me some understanding and compassion. However, when I was first counselled by him I had to have the door open, because I feared men so much. I supposed that this new therapist was going to rip all my clothes off like the other man did.

THE FIRES OF THE MIND

At the age of twenty-nine my writing career began. Despite my paralysing mood swings I wanted to become a journalist. My first article was about my famous uncle, John Fisher (Mr. Canada). He was Diefenbaker's right hand man and was Centennial Commissioner in 1967. Uncle John was a popular public speaker, book author, and eventually had his own television show. I showed the article on him to an English professor and he criticized everything about it. I cried and shoved the article in the drawer where it stayed for the next year. Finally I came to the conclusion that the worst the editor could do to me would be to reject the article and send it back, so I mailed it off to a local maritime magazine called, <u>The Atlantic Advocate.</u> I waited for a few weeks and they called me to see if I had pictures. This was a hopeful sign, so I sent them some photos. They published my article and sent me $100.00 for my effort. I got published a lot after that and wrote articles about everything from how to build a house to how to build a coffin. I worked long hours at my typewriter and went out to do interviews. I think the funniest interview I did was with an art curator. The instant I turned my tape recorder on all four of his parrots started squawking at once and his voice was completely drowned out on the cassette.

I still lived in Frosty Hollow and there was a terrible forest fire that year. Every spring the railway men would start brush fires to burn the grass away from the railway tracks and when they quit for the day they would leave the fires burning. Every since I was a kid I would go up to the tracks and put out flames with a burlap sack dunked it in the swamp. My parents went away for a couple of weeks and I was left alone in the house, terrified about the fire. I had the car right next to the door and my belongings all lined up in case I had to flee, so it was a stressful time.

KATHERINE TAPLEY-MILTON

By the time I was thirty my symptoms of mania and deep depression still dogged me. When I joined Weight Watchers I got kicked out after a short time because I evidently upstaged the lecturer. However, people would ask if I was attending the meeting, because evidently I was quite entertaining and informative. I was so manic that I constantly squirmed in my seat and spoke with pressured speech. Although I was on tons of pills, the medication in those days did not seem to control my symptoms. I had terrible panic attacks, paralytic depressions, and anxiety. One depression I remember was so bad that I lay on my side in bed for three days and three nights and couldn't even move my baby finger. I did not even have the respite of sleep to ease the suffering.

MOVING UPTOWN

The day came when my parents got too old to keep up the large farmhouse and property in Frosty Hollow, and my brother found people who wanted to rent it. We had to move fifty years of accumulated stuff in four days. I worked myself ragged, so that my father would not overexert himself and take a heart attack. At the end of the move I was hallucinating and sick physically. My father had put our old dog to sleep and all the horses had been sent to the knackers. He panicked and took cartload after cartload of stuff to dump in the woods. My artist's easel went along with the other stuff and I missed it.

The new house was modern and over insulated. It seemed without a personality compared to the rustic old house I had lived in all my life. The students that had lived in it had had chocolate pudding fights and they got it all over the walls. Everywhere there were new carpets. There was never a proper air exchange system in the house and mould grew in great quantities on the windows. A lot of my artwork and crafts went mouldy in the basement. In the living room my father turned the television to maximum volume because of his industrial deafness and my mother would turn the radio up to the limit in the kitchen. The noise was such a stress to me that I hid in my tiny bedroom for most of the time. I would cry and cut my arms in my room then wipe the tears off, hide the scars with long sleeves, and go out in the kitchen, walking on egg shells. I learned to wear a poker face when I was around my parents and people I didn't trust. The following poem describes some of my pent up emotional pain.

KATHERINE TAPLEY-MILTON

To Sleep With Anger

The rage in my bosom
Poisons my soul
Betrayed!
Betrayed!
New Wounds haemorrhage,
Old wounds fester.
Frightened by the fact
That there is no limit
On suffering,
Drowning in a sea of heartache.
Numbing the outrage
With psychotropic drugs;
Waiting for the nightmare
To cease,
But the movie reels
Turn and turn
Until I lie down
To sleep with anger.

—by Katherine Tapley-Milton

WHY DO SOME PSYCHIATRISTS ACT CRAZY?

The mental health care system sometimes reminds me of a dysfunctional family. Both are characterized by rigid roles and "shame and blame". That proved to be true when I was admitted to the Regional Hospital's psych ward shortly after we moved from the farm in Frosty Hollow. I was hospitalized to get me off of the Ativan and Xanax that I had become addicted to. Psychiatrists are the top dogs of the system and the hospital controls the lives of its inmates. The institution determines how long you stay confined, the medication you have access to, where you can go, and what time to eat and sleep.

Psychiatrists at the Regional had a bonanza labeling me. Through a student doctor I heard all of the latest labels that were affixed to me. There was a new one every day. The average mental health consumer/survivor in the province of New Brunswick has had approximately eight different diagnoses and very frequently the DMS (the psychiatrist's Bible of labels) changes definitions of the different mental illnesses. I've been called manic depressive, schizophrenic, borderline personality disorder, psychopathic, brain damaged, a case of infantile omnipotence etc. After I got out of the Regional Hospital a friend helped me cope with the confusion of what diagnosis I had by taking a piece of paper and putting a circle on it. All the different psychiatric labels were written on the outer edges of it circumference and pinned to the dart board on the wall. "Just throw a dart, see what label it lands on and that will be your type of mental illness for the day", she mockingly said.

At the Regional I was very ill from the doctor withdrawing all my medications. For three months I vomited every day and at night I could never sleep. The staff came around every hour and shone a flashlight on me and because my eyes were shut they claimed that I was sleeping. Finally, after nearly 60 days of insomnia the psychiatrist gave me a powerful hypnotic and I slept. At about 6:45 A.M. a psychiatric nurse boiled into the room and demanded that I get up immediately. The drug was so strong that I could not move a muscle. Angrily, the nurse stripped all the bedclothes off of me and stomped out.

The psychiatrist's office became a kind of kangaroo court where I was put on trial. She was a Freudian and constantly spouted terms like "a case of infantile omnipotence". The more she shamed and blamed me the more I abused myself with the scissors that they allowed me to do my crafts. I longed for someone who could look into my eyes and accept me, someone who could see my bleeding soul, but there was no compassion shown by the professionals. One day I felt so much oppression from all the shaming that I stood in the middle of the ward and sobbed, "Everybody hates me!" Half a dozen patients immediately gathered around me and collectively hugged me.

One day I packed my suitcase and was intent on leaving the hospital and running away to my friend's place. As I packed, the staff made a phone call. The next thing I knew was that a very tall, large psychiatrist stood glowering down at me. "I'll make it so that you can't leave," he threatened. That's when I became familiar with the word "certified". Legally, I was not allowed to leave the hospital for thirty days and if I had run to my friend's place the police would have come after me. I started phoning lawyers, but they wanted $1,000 in legal fees and I was broke. When I asked the hospital how I could appeal my sentence they stone-walled me.

After I got out I went to my friend's place, but she was going through a nasty divorce and was in distress herself. One night when she was really upset she kept playing the same song on the record player over and over. I took off and spent the night in a church, as I felt I could not stay there with her. That same year I had surgery to sterilize myself. I told the doctors that I could never handle having children and that I did not want to pass my illness to my progeny. I went through full abdominal surgery took a long time recovering. Eventually, I went home to my parents.

FITNESS FIASCO

I usually don't remember dates very well, but 1988 sticks out in my mind, because that's the year that the passive exercise studio opened up in town. It had machines that people were strapped into and they forced the body to exercise. There was a special on for $19.95 and I begged my mother to get me a membership. At the time I was deeply depressed, and on lithium as well as many other psychiatric drugs. I went to the exercise studio three times a week and liked it. However, I was too depressed and numb to realize that I was severely injuring my back. Eventually, I was almost passing out and lost bladder control. I ended up in adult diapers and was humiliated beyond belief. Every night I cried myself to sleep and asked God to kill me. My back was in so much agony I wasn't comfortable in any position. I saw a chiropractor, but it didn't seem to do much good. Food repulsed me and I lost a lot of weight. I went on television with my face and voice altered, because I didn't want the whole town to know it was me, and I spoke out against passive exercise studios. However, the television appearance gave me many sleepless nights and a lot of panic and anxiety.

Living in my tiny bedroom with mold growing on the windows also gave me a mold allergy and I ended up with all kinds of food sensitivities. In the end a chiropractor told me I had developed fibromyalgia. I didn't really know what that was but after looking it up on the Internet I found out that it is like Chronic Fatigue Syndrome. The immune system is compromised and there is pain in the muscles, tendons and joints. Not only did I have a mental illness, now I was living in chronic physical pain as well with two invisible diseases that few people recognize as legitimate suffering. Society seems to have a definite conception of what serious illness is comprised of. If someone has bandages or crutches or is in a wheelchair or hospital bed, then people seem to associate that with <u>real</u> illness. Invisible illness is harder to identify with and many people ignore it or minimize it.

I lived with my parents until I was in my forties because I was on a disability pension and like a lot of other mental health consumer / survivors I didn't make much money, it was a very shame-based environment, and I was very depressed and angry most of the time, however, my life was about to change in a radical way.

THE DAY MY FATHER DIED

It was early morning, around 8 a.m., and I was still asleep. However, I was awakened by the sounds of crying by my bedroom door. My mother simply said, "He's gone. He's gone." She grabbed me and hugged me and told me that we had to be strong. My mind reeled in disbelief as I went into my parents' bedroom and saw my father lying there. He looked like he was asleep and I refused to believe my mother. Then I touched his body and there was an unnatural coldness to it. His face was a grey death mask. It was then I realized that my father was dead.

I then went into my bedroom and dialled "911". I was crying as I told them, "My father is dead." In the next five minutes the house began filling with police and ambulance workers. I was still sobbing and all I wanted to do was to sit there and say "Goodbye" to my father, but they asked for his medications and went through the mechanics of their job. It seemed that they wanted to get the body out of the house as soon as possible. They kept trying to get me to leave the room, but I had to touch my father just one last time. It seemed that the professionals wanted to stifle my tears and my grief. If I had to do it over again I don't think I would have called "911" so soon.

Only an hour after my father's body was out of the house, the food started pouring in. It was hard to put on a front for the neighbours who brought sandwiches, casseroles, etc. In fact I was so deep in grief that I felt insulted that people could actually contemplate eating at a time like this. But it always has amazed me at how ravenously hungry people get around the time of a funeral.

Soon after the food arrived, the relatives started coming and the house was packed. I just wanted to sit in my room crying, and let my grief be private, but I felt like I was on display in a fishbowl. I hadn't had anyone this close to me die before, so I didn't know what to expect. My friend drove me uptown to get my pills at the drugstore and I was composed while in the car. However, in the drugstore I met the mayor of the town and tried to tell her about my father's passing. I broke down completely, the image of my father, so grey and so cold still vivid in my mind.

One of my friends took charge of me and asked if I would like to speak with a lady who had lost her father a couple of months before. She was farther along in the grief stages than I was. We talked for hours and I cried. She said that the funeral was the worst day for her. However, my own grief journey was to be different than hers.

As the guest and relatives milled around the kitchen at my house I listed to some soft Celtic music and tried to come to grips with my loss. The first night was dreadful as I saw my father's death mask over and over. I had to call a counsellor at 11 P.M. and take extra medication to get to sleep.

My father's death was sudden and he wasn't even sick the night before, there were so many things that I wanted to say to him but couldn't. I came up with the idea of writing a letter to him and putting it in his grave. I told him I loved him and how I was sorry for any wrongs I had done him. I also expressed my hope that he was in heaven and at peace with himself. The first time I read the letter to one of my friends, I sobbed uncontrollably, but by the time I got to the third or fourth paragraph I had gotten a lot of the grief out.

I dreaded the day of the funeral, because I expected it to be the hardest part of the grief, but surprisingly it wasn't. The country church was packed with his friends and relations, flowers lined the wall, and his favourite hymn, "Farther Along" was sung. Compared to the morning I found my father dead the funeral was a lot easier. Since my father chose to be cremated there was no viewing of the body. My family thinks that open caskets are barbaric, but I think they serve a purpose of saying goodbye to the physical aspect of the deceased. However, in retrospect perhaps I was luckier than the rest of the family as I saw the physical reality of my father lying dead in his bed. I knew without question that he was gone, although I went through a lot of emotional trauma at first.

After the funeral I was puzzled by the reaction I got from people on the street. Living in a small town of 6,000 people news travels fast and my father's obituary was in at least two newspapers. However, I noticed that people wouldn't talk about my father. I'd asked if they knew he had passed away and the inevitable answer was a "Yes". However, they avoided the topic if they could. It seems that after the funeral is over, society expects the grief to be over as well. But of course the grief had just begun.

I attempted to deal with my grief by reading books on the grieving process, listened to tapes, and talked to a counsellor. The most significant statement I remember reading is that "grief is the price we pay for love". My father and I had a turbulent relationship, but the depth of grief I felt over his passing proved that my love for him was real. As I placed the tear stained letter in the grave after the urn went in, I finally felt that I had said, "Goodbye."

THE SOLITARY LIFE

My father's death opened up a new chapter in my life. I was kicked out of my mother's house due to a misunderstanding of something I had said to my brother and began to live life alone in an apartment. It was a one bedroom apartment and had very poor temperature control in it. At times I felt like I was frying because of the intense heat and other times in the winter the pipes would freeze up and there would be no heat at all. I remember having a bad cold when there wasn't any heat and I piled every blanket that I could find on top of myself. However, I have never been so cold in all my life. I might just as well have been outdoors.

Shortly after I moved into the apartment I went to the S.P.C.A. and picked out an orange tabby cat. I called him "Sir Lancelot" because I wanted a knight in shining armour to protect and love me. The cat was in terrible shape when I got him. He was starved, had mites in his ears, and had a tapeworm. However, from the first, we developed a psychic bond with each other and Sir Lancelot is still a big comfort to me. He seems to sense my moods and comforts me when I am down, even licking the tears from my cheeks when I cry.

During the time I lived alone in the apartment I had a couple of disturbing incidents happened that still bother me to this day. One incident occurred when I was feeling very suicidal and the voices in my head were demanding that I take an overdose. I called the provincial help line and while I was talking on the phone with a counsellor, there was a knock on the door and two burly policemen came in. The police talked with me for about 10 minutes and then demanded that I accompany them to the local hospital. I had no choice but to comply. Alone in the backseat of the police car I felt shamed and humiliated. What was I a criminal that I had to be placed there? I was ill not breaking the law. I felt degraded.

Another disturbing incident was when the Native Canadian I knew from my Centracare days started calling me on the phone. I was very lonely and felt flattered with all the male attention. After a few phone calls he wanted to visit me in person. All seemed to go well until I realized that his Native religion and my Christianity did not mix. When I decided to break off the relationship he threatened me and I had to call the police. I knew that he carried guns and knives on him, because I had seen them in his pack. I thought that he would come and kill me.

Later, I met his ex wife. She said that he had shot at her and his children. All the while I knew this guy he had maintained that he worked as a spy for the Canadian government. His ex wife thought that was just fantasy, however, I must say that he maintained that spy story for 25 years, so who knows, maybe it was true? Even today he still calls on the phone from time to time but doesn't speak.

MIRACLES OCCUR IN THE STRANGEST OF PLACES

After I had lived alone for two years and been single and celebrate for at least ten years I felt hat I would be an 'old maid' or 'spinster' for the rest of my life. It seemed that in a society made for couples being single and lonely made me an aberration. One day when I was on the Internet I had placed a description of myself on a site called, "Adam Meet Eve", a Christian dating club. As time went on I forgot about the ad. However, I suddenly got an email from a man in Saint John named Dave. At first he was reluctant to meet me, having had bad experiences with women in the past. However, before we knew it the emails turned into phone calls and the phone calls turned into visits. Dave suffers from a neurological disease called "Dystonia" or Spasmodic Torticollis, which makes his neck muscles go into spasms. I took the bus to visit him in Saint John one weekend and he came to visit me in my apartment on alternate weekends. I couldn't drive to Saint John due to my panic attacks and Dave couldn't drive because of his Dystonia. Soon, the like turned into love. One Christmas we were snowed in and spent a lot of time together in my apartment. In true feminist fashion I proposed to Dave and he said 'yes'.

I started planning the wedding in January of 2001 and made a lot of the flowers and decorations myself. On June 2nd Dave and I were married in the Mount Allison Chapel and had our honeymoon at the Amherst Shore Inn, in Nova Scotia. I marvelled constantly about the fact that despite the fact that I was mentally ill, Dave loved me anyway. In the past I had always thought that I would never find a man who would accept me as I am. Today we have been married almost five years and we have had many challenges coping with our illnesses.

I still have crises from time to time and have to have intervention from the Mental Health Clinic. Despite the voices, the anxiety, and depressions, I have always believed that as a handicapped person I should live as normal a life as possible and be integrated into society. I have often struggled with the meaninglessness of my mental illness, however, a psychologist pointed out that my main purpose is to be a mental health advocate. He also said that persons who do advocacy don't reach their full potential until they are sixty, so I guess I have ten more years to go.

EPILOGUE
BIRD ON A WIRE

I am still in the process of recovering from mental illness and the institutional, sexual, and verbal abuse that I have suffered. A friend that has known me for more than twenty years says that I am a totally different person than when she first met me. She remembers driving me home when I was totally manic and I was eating carrots as fast as I could and spitting out the tops. Things that have been instrumental in my ongoing recovery are support from my friends, talking to therapists, exercise, getting adequate sleep, medications, and networking with other consumer/survivors.

Successfully managing psychiatric illness is like being a bird on a wire in a violent windstorm. Because of the biochemical disorder that I have, I never know what mood I'll wake up in. Some days I'm energetic, upbeat, and productive, and other days I'm depressed, anguished, have feelings of utter worthlessness, and become actively suicidal.

It still bothers me that I feel I have to sweep everything under the rug for society. Some people gawk at the scars on my arm and make ignorant comments. Also, I know that some employers won't hire me because of my mental illness. One time a bipolar person commented, "It would be better for you if you were in a wheelchair, then people would know that there's something wrong with you and have some sympathy." I find it very frustrating dealing with an invisible illness. Many persons believe that will power alone will overcome emotional illness, but I have never found that to work on eradicating my symptoms. Also, positive self-talk does not work on the voices I hear. In fact, the more I try to shout down the voices, the more aggressive they become. The only thing I can do is to try to distract myself with music, the radio, or some kind of activity.

Being a curious and experimental person has led me down many paths to seek a cure for my mental illness. I've tried out many health food diets, megavitamins, herbs, and a myriad of alternative medicine treatments. However, I still have to be maintained on medication and psychotherapy. I'd love to walk into the psychologist's office and say, "My mind is no longer full of scorpions, I'm cured!" However, I know that every day will be a struggle with mental anguish. I once met a lady in her sixties that had both schizophrenia and cancer and she told me, "The mental and spiritual darkness that I've suffered with the schizophrenia is far more painful than the cancer."

I hope that in reading my book you have a better understanding of those of us who live in the shadow lands of serious emotional illness. We need more humane care in hospitals, and true understanding and support from the public. Right now life insurance companies will not insure mental health consumer/survivors and shock therapy, that I've observed to be very damaging to individuals, is more popular with the psychiatrists than ever. I'd like to have members of the public get up in arms and help us fight for our rights. Let's stop the barbarism and treat mental health consumer/survivors as descent human beings.

Thank you for reading my book.

APPENDIX: SONGS, ARTICLES, POEMS, SOURCES OF HELP

A. A SHORT PSYCHIATRIC HISTORY LESSON

From The Annals Of Psychiatric Absurdity

Rhazes the Arabian Doctor

From A.D. 865 to 925, Rhazes was an Arabian doctor who was considered to be an outstanding scholar of the times. He wrote over 200 different volumes on medicine, religion, philosophy, and astronomy. As he rose to prominence, he became physician-in-chief to the Baghdad Hospital, which was a remarkable institution of its time, because it had a ward exclusively for the mentally ill. Rhazes saw the body/mind connection with mental illness and even used a primitive form of psychotherapy. However, the Arabian doctor ran afoul of the other influential doctors who believed that all illness was the result of demon activity. Since Rhazes disagreed with the medical establishment he was sentenced "to be hit over the head with his own book, until the book or the head broke." This early psychiatrist was rendered blind after this punishment. (Taken from The History of Psychiatry by Franz. G. Alexander and Sheldon T. Selesnick)

Suicides Punished in Medieval Times

The act of suicide was extremely repugnant to the medieval mind. Those who killed themselves had extreme punishments carried on their corpses to enact symbolic shame. The book, Legal Lore, by William Andrews explains that, "The body was, by the customary law ... to be drawn to the gibbet (instrument of hanging) as cruelly as possible ... . The very door-step of the house in which he lay was to be torn up, for the dead man was not worthy to pass over it.

Impalement, transfixture by a stake, though well enough known on the continent as a punishment for the living, became there (in France) and in England alike, the special doom of the suicide."

<u>Psychotic Mass Movement in Medieval Times</u>

During the 13th and 14th centuries mass movements arose, driving many psychotic. In Hungary, in the year 1231 a cult arose that believed that the plague was caused by personal sins. <u>The History of Psychiatry</u> says that, "They marched through Europe singing hymns, bearing red crosses on their breasts, and carrying whips with knots from which hung iron tongs." They were known as "flagellants" and their converts whipped themselves in public. Although their group was condemned by Pope Clement, another group of flagellants sprang up in Strasbourg in 1418.

B. THE THINKIN' SONG

Originally written by Bob Janes
Sung by Steve Fobert on "Alive on Arrival"

Chorus:
Well don't you go thinkin'
And thinkin' and thinkin'
And thinkin' so much 'till
You're stranded behind.
Don't you go thinkin'
And thinkin' and thinkin'
Thinkin' so much that
You're losin' your mind.

There's many depressions
All ploughed in your brain
Trace them too far and they'll
Drive you insane.
You're twisted so tight now
You can hardly talk
Get out in the daylight and go for a walk.

Chorus:

All the tension inside you
Has gone to your face
You're flashin' your madness
All over the place.
You stand in the hallway

And try to explain
I look in your eyes and see shackles and chains.

Chorus:

You're chasin' some notion you've misunderstood
You're tryin' so hard, can't your see it's no good?
You analyze everything into a "No"
You're falling apart you've got nothing to show.

Chorus:

C. SOME ARTICLES ON MENTAL ILLNESS

1.
Famous Mentally Ill Persons

The view that the general public has of the mentally ill is mostly negative. This has been largely shaped by the media and movies that have portrayed the mentally ill as undesirable, dangerous individuals, preying on society. In an article titled, "The Criminalization of the Mentally Ill", by David Gonzalez, he states, "Movies such as *Maniac (1934), Deranged (1974), Psycho (1960),* and *The Lunatic (1992),* all portray the mentally ill as psychotic and deranged lunatics capable of snapping at the slightest provocation. Movies such as these add to the misconceptions of the mentally ill and eventually influence the opinions of the judges, district attorneys, police officers, parole officers, correction officers, politicians, and the average citizen".

Society's stigma about mental illness indicates the failure to recognize that some of the people who have made the greatest contributions to society have suffered from mental health problems. The list of famous mentally ill persons is surprisingly extensive. It includes names like Abraham Lincoln, Virginia Woolf, Michelangelo, Winston Churchill, Charles Dickens, Patty Duke, and John Forbes Nash. The following short biographies represent a walk through the mental illness hall of fame.

<u>Abraham Lincoln</u>

The famous sixteenth president of the United States, Abraham Lincoln (1809-1865) brought to politics his personal integrity, intelligence, and humanity. He was called the "Great Emancipator" because of his stand against slavery. However, Lincoln suffered severe and incapacitating depressions that occasionally led to thoughts of suicide. The Encyclopedia Americana concludes that, "Although his reputation has fluctuated with changing times, he was clearly a great man and a great president. He firmly and fairly guided the nation through its most perilous period and made a lasting impact in shaping the office of chief executive." In the many listings of famous mentally ill persons, Abraham Lincoln is always present at the top.

Virginia Woolf

Even fifty years after her suicide by drowning, Virginia Woolf's writing continues to be a source of influence. The International Virginia Woolf Society Web Page comments, "Woolf has since been recognized as one of the most important and influential feminist writers of the twentieth century and as a writer whose works are dynamically engaged with the political, philosophical, historical and materialist issues of her time." Scholars continue to be stimulated by Woolf's writings, even though in her private life she was tortured by bipolar illness.

Winston Churchill

Sir Winston Churchill (1874-1965) suffered from what he called his "black dog" of depression and it has been said, "Had he been a stable and equable man, he could never have inspired the nation. In 1940, when all the odds were against Britain, a leader of sober judgment might well have concluded that we were finished." He became the voice of Britain during the war and gave emotional speeches inspiring England to endure hardship and sacrifice in order to prevail over Germany. Along with being a famous politician Churchill also was an accomplished writer and painter. In 1953 he was awarded the Nobel Prize for Literature for his six volume history of World War II. Also, he wrote the four volume "History of the English-speaking Peoples". Churchill achieved fame despite being bipolar.

MIND FULL OF SCORPIONS

Charles Dickens

Although he was one of the greatest authors in the English language, Charles Dickens (1812-1870) suffered from clinical depression. At 17 he worked as a court stenographer and later as a parliamentary reporter. By 1833 his literary sketches of London life were becoming famous. His classic novels such as "Oliver Twist", "Nicholas Nickleby" and "The Old Curiousity Shop" became the most popular of his day. Dickens was supremely successful at portraying the sights, sounds, smells, and customs of nineteenth Century London. He blasted the social inequality and injustices of his day and brought attention to the plight of the downtrodden. Although some critics feel his work is disorderly and sentimental none can doubt his genius at revealing real life.

Patty Duke

Born in 1946, Patty Duke also called Anna Duke suffered the ravages of bipolar illness, anorexia, and substance abuse until she got diagnosed and put on lithium. She made many suicide attempts and even though she could always perform well as an actress her personal life was turbulent. Duke was the youngest actress ever to have her own show and had a twelve inch doll made like her, along with a Patty Duke game for teenagers. At the age of twelve she starred in "The Miracle Worker", the story of Helen Keller. She became the youngest actress to win an Oscar award.

Many television awards later, Patty Duke is a spokesperson for the mentally ill and has written the book, "A Brilliant Madness" to help those suffering from bipolar disorder.

Michelangelo

Michelangelo Buonarroti was born near Florence, Italy in 1495 and died at the age of 89. His name is synonymous with his famous sculptures and paintings done during the Renaissance period. His most famous sculpture is "David" which stands 16 feet 10 inches tall, and the painting he is best known for is his rendering of the

Sistine Chapel. He is still known as a giant in the art world even though he suffered the symptoms of bipolar illness.

John Forbes Nash, Jr.

John Forbes Nash won the Nobel Prize for pioneering work in game theory on October 11th, 1994. That was unusual because most of his life he had suffered from paranoid schizophrenia. At www.schizophrenia.com it is noted that, "There are relatively few famous people with schizophrenia." Indeed the preponderance of famous mentally ill persons are bipolar. John Nash began his PhD at Princeton in 1948 when he was twenty years old. He wrote a doctoral thesis on the mathematics of competition that is still used today. He dazzled the mathematical world and invented the game called "Hex" put out by Parker Brothers. However, for twenty-five years he was immersed in schizophrenia. His mathematical theories did not make sense and he looked for secret messages in numbers. Somehow in the mid 1980's his illness went into remission and he is now working on novel uses of the computer at Princeton.

Buzz Aldrin

On July 20th, 1969 Buzz Aldrin and Neil Armstrong were the first human beings to set foot on the moon witnessed by the largest television audience in history. Buzz was born in Monclair, New Jersey, the son of an aviation pilot. He received his doctorate of astronautics from the Massachusetts Institute of Technology. The techniques that Buzz developed were used on all of NASA's missions, including the first space docking with the Russian Cosmonauts. In 1993 he received a patent for a permanent space station he designed. Buzz is also the author of two space novels titled The Return and Encounter with Tiber. He is also authoring his autobiography. Despite his fame, Buzz Aldrin is bipolar.

Robin Williams

Robin Williams was born on July 21, 1952 in Chicago Illinois.

He studied political science, then went into acting at Julliard Acting Academy. His first break came in 1978 when he played Mork on Happy Days. The next step was for Williams was his first TV show Mork and Mindy, in which the character of Mork became very popular. His first movie was in 1986 and was called Popeye. It was a failure. However, a year later Good Morning America was a big success. He has also gone on to act in Good Will Hunting, Dead Poet's Society, Jacob the Liar, Mrs. Doubtfire, Patch Adams, Awakenings, and in 1997 was voted the funniest man alive by Entertainment Weekly. Williams has also won an Oscar. Behind the scenes, Robin Williams has struggled with attention deficit disorder and cocaine addiction.

Conclusion

It should be evident by now that throughout history that some of the most influential individuals have suffered from mental illness. In the field of art, politics, writing, and acting there have been geniuses who were afflicted by inner torments. Yet despite this hindrance and pain they rose to greatness. It is time that society realizes the great debt that it owes to the mentally ill, instead of portraying them all as killers and monsters.

2.
FAMOUS ONLY IN THE MIND: AN INSIGHT INTO PSYCHOSIS

I am indeed a very famous and adored creature. There are so many times have played Spanish guitar or done pop concerts in packed out auditoriums in all the top cities. The number of books I've written is phenomenal and of course each one has been accompanied by a tour of all the T.V. talk shows. Experts seek my advice constantly on subjects ranging from religion to politics. Each movie that I have starred in has been a huge success at the box office and of course my love life couldn't be better. I have written many screen plays which have received Academy awards and I'm never seen in public with a hair out of place or a broken nail. My make up is flawless and my complexion gorgeous. Women everywhere envy my perfect figure and I never sweat. But, alas I am all this only in my own mind. Fantasy or "wool gathering" as some people like to refer to it can be wonderful. When the vice of cruel reality crushes the hope out of me I have always tended to escape to a world of my own creation. It's a dream like world where lovers never hurt you and pie is never fattening. The beaches are always sunny and the water is always 72 degrees. A little crisis is always met with a knight in shining armor who pledges his allegiance and fidelity forever. Gravity never hurts anyone and the whole world gets saved and goes to heaven. The down side of fantasy is that you can come to like it so much that reality becomes bland, banal, and noxious by comparison. I find fantasy can be so addictive that I would like to cancel my environment in favor of prime time fantasy. For someone with a vivid imagination it's better than television. However, unless one wants to give oneself completely over to fantasy and live in a mental institution the world with its frustrations and agonies must be met with courage, with fortitude, with compassion. A little fantasy can be the spice of life, however it is a dangerous obsession. Some take the trip of fantasy and never come back.

3.
HUMOR THAT CAN HURT OR HEAL

Hurtful Humour

I think that the mentally ill are the last group of persons left that can be mocked and made fun of without it being considered politically incorrect. In today's society it's considered in poor taste to make racist jokes or wise cracks about sexual orientation, but it's still open season on the mentally ill. The following two jokes taken from Internet sources demonstrate my point.

Joke Example # 1

"A doctor at the asylum decided to take his inmates to a baseball game. For weeks in advance, he coached his patients to his commands. When the day of the game arrived, everything seemed to be going well. As the national anthem started,

The doctor yelled, "Up nuts!" And the inmates complied by standing up. After the anthem he yelled, "Down nuts!" And they all sat. After a home run he yelled, "Cheer nuts!" And they all broke into applause and cheers. Thinking things were going very well, he decided to go get a beer and a hot dog, leaving his assistant in charge. When he returned there was a riot in progress. Finding the assistant, he asked what happened. The assistant replied, "Well ... everything was fine until some guy walked by and yelled, "PEANUT!"

Joke Example # 2

It was visitor's day at the lunatic asylum. All the inmates were standing in the courtyard and singing "Ave Maria". And singing it beautifully. Oddly, each of them was holding a red apple in one hand and tapping it rhythmically with a pencil. A visitor listened in wonderment to the performance and then approached the choir. "I am a retired choir director," he said. "This is one of the best choirs I have ever heard." "Yes, I'm very proud of them," said the conductor. "You should take them on tour," said the visitor. "What are they called?" "Surely that is obvious", replied the conductor, "the Moron Tap-an-apple Choir."

Calling the mentally ill "nuts, and morons" and referring to a mental hospital as a lunatic asylum is hurtful and degrading. In a column by Otto Wahl Ph.D. he comments: "People whose self-esteem may already be compromised by their disorders see themselves being laughed at and misrepresented. They are aware that other serious conditions are seldom treated with such insensitivity and wonder what they have done to warrant such treatment. They may also be angered and discouraged by the apparent lack of sympathy for their concerns and being the target of such ridicule. Moreover, humor that ridicules those with mental illness reinforces the public's already pronounced tendencies to disparage those with mental illness and treat them with disrespect. While people who enjoy status and social acceptance may be able to accept humor at their expense, those who have long been stigmatized, devalued, and discriminated against cannot afford to be tolerant."

I think that it is high time that psychiatric survivors should protest abusive humor directed at us. How many times a week do you hear mental illness referred to in a derogatory way? Without thinking people use hurtful humor. Words like psycho, nutbar, looney tunes, crazy, bonkers, etc. slip from the tongues of many every day, offending millions of persons afflicted with the agony of mental illness. Psychiatric survivors should refuse to accept slurs on their condition even if people hide by saying, "It's just a joke." To report instances of stigma in the media, an individual can call 800-969-NMHA (National Mental Health Association) or to subscribe to NMHA's Stigma Watch Alerts you can visit their website at www.nmha.org and click on "Online Community".

Healing Humour

A century ago Sigmund Freud recognized that humor offers us a healthy escape from stress. Comedian, Groucho Marx, observed that, "If it weren't for the brief respite we give the world with our foolishness, the world would see mass suicide in numbers that compare favorably with the death of lemmings." Furthermore, Paul E. McGhee in an article titled, "Humor Your Tumor", states that: "Your sense of humor is one of the most powerful tools you have to make certain that your daily mood and emotional state support good health, instead of working against it." Psychotherapist and stand-up comedian David Grenirer, advises: "Here's a tip for the nest time you feel stressed out and need a wellness break. It's called the Smile Time Out. Take a deep breath, smile, exhale and say, 'Aaah' while visualizing all your muscles and cells smiling. Then add to that a memory of a time you felt really good and laughed and laughed. Remember, even when you fake a smile or laugh, you get the same physiological benefits as when it's the real thing, because your mind is smart, but your body is stupid and can't tell the difference." I can't imagine this working with someone who is deeply depressed, however, for those mildly to moderately glum it might have some benefit.

In his article, "Humor in Group Therapy", therapist Tony J. Joyner attests to the healing power of humor. He comments, "By increasing the client's enjoyment of and participation in his / her treatment, a therapeutic environment permissive of light-hearted discussion and laughter can positively affect treatment outcome. I found this to be true through my 14+ years of work as a mental health professional. I currently work with adult and adolescent psychiatric patients in an acute care unit and incorporate humor into my one-to-one sessions and my game or group presentations on a regular basis. I found through the use of appropriately timed humor that I developed a quick rapport and a lighter group atmosphere. This opens up opportunities for therapeutic interventions. It gives patients a friendly and human touch that they need during this difficult and frightening time in their lives."

There is a need breed of therapist today called a "jollyologist" or one who specializes in humor. You can actually get a Masters Degree in the subject. Allen Klein, creator of the show Captain Kangaroo has hit the road as a professional jollyologist and has authored books such as "Up Words For Down Days" and "The Courage to Laugh". Whether one is dealing with a traffic jam or a tragedy Klein teaches people to use humor to soften the blow. Patch Adams is an unconventional doctor who sports a red rubber nose and a whoopee cushion instead stethoscope. He believes that laughter is the best medicine and is another jollyologist with his own particular quirks.

Humor has the power to hurt as well as heal. While psychiatric survivors may be wounded by insensitive jokes and slang references to our illness, thus minimizing our pain, humor in therapy or in our personal lives can lighten our black moods and give us a sense of control over our lives.

4.
TMS: AN ALTERNATIVE TO ELECTROSHOCK

Shock therapy is back in vogue among psychiatrists, a fact which I find very disturbing. While the doctors claim it helps depression and is safe, in reality shock therapy can have the side effect of long term or short-term memory damage that in a lot of cases can be permanent. An alternative therapy, TMS or "Transcranial Magnetic Stimulation" seems to be a less barbaric treatment that does not cause brain damage. General anesthetic is not required with TMS and specific areas of the brain can be targeted without causing a convulsion.

According to the National Alliance for Research on Schizophrenia and Depression, TMS " ... has been successful in helping people who are severely depressed." TMS uses an external magnet to stimulate the left prefrontal cortex, an area of the brain that is found to be functioning abnormally in depressed individuals. Dr. Mark George comments, "This new tool allows us for the first time in the history of mankind to stimulate the brain while the person is awake and alert." In a study of 30 depressed, suicidal patients who had not been helped by medication, 20 had TMS for 20 minutes five days a week for a fortnight. Ten patients had the magnetic device placed on their heads but didn't receive the treatment. None of the patients knew if they received the real treatment or not. The patients who received the TMS therapy showed a marked improvement in their depression, while the controls showed no improvement at all. Apparently, the only side effect of TMS is that a third of the patients reported a mild headache, which was easily relieved with common over the counter remedies like ibuprophen.

The biological mechanisms that trigger depression are still not well known, however, research done using MRI machines has detected abnormalities in the prefrontal cortex of depressed patients. This reason lead scientists to consider TMS as a tool to target that area. Before TMS becomes a standard treatment for depression at your local Mental Health Clinic, more studies have to be done to determine why it works, what intensity of magnetic power to use, and how frequent the treatment should be. However, Dr. George feels that further MRI research will reveal more of the brains secrets. Also, there is controversy over whether a treatment which does not cause a convulsion is as effective as electroshock which does cause a convulsion. Traditional electroshock requires anesthesia and this can produce over sedation and vomiting afterwards, while TMS does not have these discomforts.

There are a significant number of depressed patients who are not helped by antidepressants or experience too unpleasant side effects to tolerate them. While there is still experimentation going on with TMS it has been around for ten years and looks like a humane and viable alternative to shock therapy. Personally, I would run as fast as I could away from having shock therapy, but I would gladly submit to being treated with TMS.

5.
SCHIZOAFFECTIVE DISORDER

Of all the categories of psychiatric illness, schizoaffective disorder has the distinction of being the most complex and controversial. . This mental illness seems to be neither fish nor fowl, but a mixture of mood disorder and schizophrenic symptoms. At Mentalwellness.com the experts say, "People suffering from schizoaffective disorder experience a chronic roller-coaster ride of symptoms and problems that may be more difficult to cope with than either of its parent diseases, schizophrenia or affective disorders (formerly known as mood disorders.) .

THE HUMAN FACE OF THE ILLNESS

J. from Moncton, New Brunswick, has schizoaffective disorder. She suffers a lot of mental anguish and has to live in a special care home. Her first episode of the illness started when she was 23 year old when she was working at a restaurant. She had to be hospitalized. J. says, "I felt scared, paranoid." Her second breakdown occurred in her thirties. She remembers, "I was really sick. What happened was I was working doing some housework for my aunt. I looked at the wall and there was this big hole. I saw Jesus and His hair was moving. I hallucinated. I saw snow inside the house. In the sky I saw a horse with wings ... I was scared to go out in the public. I had anxiety attacks. I had a prayer in my hand and I told my parents that I was going to heaven and they said, 'That 's it we're taking you to the hospital." (The doctor) told me that I was schizoaffective with a chemical imbalance." She complains of insomnia and nightmares along with the hallucinations, anxiety attacks, depressions, suicidal episodes, and of fear.

The voices in her head tell her to kill people, but she strongly fights the urge.

J. spends her days going to two activity centres for the mentally ill and at night the staff at the special care home supervise her.

SCHIZOAFFECTIVE DISORDER DEFINED

The basic definition of schizoaffective disorder that guides the professionals is the DMS-IV description of the illness. The DSM-IV diagnostic criteria lists three basic requirements for schizoaffective disorder. These are "A. An uninterrupted period of illness which, at some time, there is either a major depressive episode, a manic episode, or a mixed episode concurrent with symptoms that meet Criterion A for schizophrenia (delusions, hallucinations, disorganized speech, grossly disorganized behaviour or catatonia, and negative symptoms such as affect flattening) B. During the same period of illness, there have been delusions or hallucinations for at least 2 weeks in the absence of prominent mood symptoms. C. Symptoms that meet criteria for a mood episode are present for a substantial portion of the total duration of the active and residual periods of the illness." A schizophrenic may experience depression in the aftermath of a psychotic episode, but the thought and mood disorder are not concurrent. " Jacques Gallant, a psychiatric nurse who works in Moncton at the Mental Health Clinic comments, "When you see a schizophrenic person you see a person with delusions and hallucinations mostly. Not saying that schizoaffective disorder does not have that, but that this is not the main feature of the illness. " Gallant also mentions that the depression or mania would be of longer duration in a person with schizoaffective disorder.

<u>AN OVERVIEW OF TREATMENT OPTIONS</u>

Untreated schizoaffective disorder can leave the victim homeless, alone, and without money, so that along with the medications the patient also needs housing, psychotherapy, community support, and recreational opportunities. Since schizoaffective disorder appears to be a combination of thought disorder, mood disorder, and anxiety disorder the medication regime given is usually a combination of anti-psychotic, antidepressant, and anti-anxiety drugs. Psychiatric nurse, Jacques Gallant comments: "If the person is in a manic state then you would give mood stabilizers. If the person is in a psychotic state, then you would give anti-psychotics. Usually most of the time you would combine the two treatments together if it's clearly known that the person suffers from schizoaffective disorder." Gallant goes on to mention that mood stabilizers like Epival, Lithium, Tegretol are often used along with minor tranquilizers like Clonazipam, and atypical anti-psychotics like Olanzapine.

J. is on transene (a seditive), Lamactal (a mood stabilizer), Effecxor (an anti-depressant, and resperiodol (an anti-psychotic). Some patients who are noncompliant with the drug therapy end up taking long acting injectable drugs such as Haldol, Pipotiazine, or Fluphenazine. Dr. Phillip W. Long (www.mentalhealth.com) cautions against using the older antidepressants, as he feels they worsen schizoaffective disorder.

In acute phases of the illness the patient may need 24 hour care in a hospital or a residential setting. However, the goal is to integrate the person back into the community as soon as possible and to encourage independent living. Some individuals with this illness manage to work.

CONCLUSION

The National Alliance for the Mentally Ill (NAMI) states that "Because schizoaffective disorder is so complicated, misdiagnoses is common. Some people may be misdiagnosed as having schizophrenia. Others may be misdiagnosed as having bipolar disorder. As a practical matter, differentiating between schizophrenia, bipolar disorder, and schizoaffective disorder is not absolutely critical, since anti psychotic medication is recommended for all three ... The prognosis for individuals diagnosed with schizoaffective disorder is generally better than for those diagnosed with schizophrenia, but not quite as good for those diagnosed with a mood disorder." Although schizoaffective disorder is challenging for the therapist and agonizing for the patient the advent of newer, atypical anti psychotics seem to be more comfortable for the patient and provide a brighter outlook for the future.

SELF HELP

What can the patient do to make the best possible recovery? Information from the New York Presbyterian Hospital states that the person should do the following:

—Accept that you have a prolonged illness

—Identify your strengths and limitations

—Make clear realistic goals

—After a relapse, go slowly and gradually back to your responsibilities.

—Plan a regular, consistent, predictable daily routine.

—Make your home as quiet, calm and relaxed as you can.

—Identify and reduce stress. Make only one change in you life at a time.

—Work toward an active and trusting relationship with the staff involved in you care.

—Take your medicines regularly, as prescribed.

—Identify early signs of relapse. Make your own early warning list.

—Get involved with a group of people you feel comfortable with.

—Avoid street drugs.

—With or not you drink alcohol is a very personal decision you should make with your prescriber.

—Eat a well balanced diet.

—Get enough rest.

—Get regular exercise.

—If you're not sure whether your feelings or fears are based in reality, ask someone you trust or compare your behaviour with others.

—Accept that there may be setbacks from time to time.

On the Internet many links that provide information on

schizoaffective disorder can be found at http://www.psycom.net/ depression.central.schizoaffective.html .

6.
WHAT IS MISSING IN THE SYSTEM?

Recently, I was hospitalized and since have been pondering what is missing in the formal mental health care system. I was in a personal crisis when I decided to see if the hospitals have changed in the last 18 years since I was incarcerated the last time. Indeed, I was willing to go in open-minded and see for myself. My husband and I waited for hours in a grubby little room at outpatients and noted that a man with chest pains was immediately rushed in for treatment. The first lesson was that a mental health crisis is put on the back burner compared to other diseases. After seeing the psychiatrist, I was processed and put in the belly of the beast. My personal belongings were rummaged through and all my pills were confiscated. I was feeling violated, but still entertained the possibility of getting help.

The thing that came next was a shot in the butt. This, I was told, was supposed to help make the withdrawal from antidepressants smooth and painless. For the next 72 hours I was supposed to sleep. It didn't quite happen like that though. I lay on a lumpy bed and was given so many doses of Zyprexa that my restless leg syndrome made me pace the halls in physical torment. I found myself treated like a bad child and subjected to silly, inconsistent, and petty rules. Although I am nearly 50 years old and have survived fires, floods and everything in between I was not allowed down in the hospital lobby to get a Tim Horton's coffee. This was supposed to be behavior modification, but what was the objective? To make me a trained seal that flapped my flippers on command? There was an absence of being treated with dignity and no respect for my surviving a life of so much pain. Instead of the harbor of safety that I sought, the hospital was a police state complete with video cameras to watch my every move.

My expectations of being hospitalized were that I would receive counseling, occupational therapy, and group therapy. On my own initiative I went once to group therapy and to crafts, but did not receive any form of counseling. (It was explained to me that I was too upset to get counseling). The group therapy revealed a half dozen consumers who all said that they had no hope left. It was obvious that the system was not meeting their needs, but leading them to despair. In my opinion some common sense, compassion, and caring would have made the difference. I have attended many consumer groups in different parts of the country and felt compassion, concern, comfort, and inner healing, however, the hospital seemed to have no soul. The routine seemed to reduce individuals to mere cogs in a wheel. I was not treated like a person with dignity, but a thing to be pushed around. Essentially, all the experience did was make me angry and outraged. In the end I have concluded that the hospital system is no more enlightened than it was 18 years ago and a place to be avoided like the Plague.

An American National Research Project for the Development of Recovery Facilitating System Performance Indicators sponsored by nine different states comments that: "We must fully acknowledge that the formal system often hinders recovery through the bureaucratic program guidelines, limited access to services and supports, abusive practices, poor quality services, negative messages, lack of 'best practice' program elements, and a narrow focus on a bio-psychiatric orientation that can actually serve to discount the person's humanity and ignore other practical, psychological, social, and spiritual human needs. At the core of such hindering forces is the operationalization of society's response to mental illness, that of shame and hopelessness and the need to assert social control over the unknown and uncomfortable."

This same National Research Project which I found on the Internet (www.namiscc.org/ Recovery/2002MentalHealthRecovery.

htm) points out that recovery for consumers/survivors points to many universal components, some of which the system could help provide if it had the will. Those who have material resources such as a livable income, safe housing, healthcare, transportation, and a telephone do better than those who live in poverty, and a lack of basic resources. Attitudes of fear, shame, lack of personal responsibility, self loathing, and invalidation impede recovery, whereas recovery chances are boosted if the system encourages self-reliance, personal resourcefulness, self-advocacy, choices in treatment and a holistic view of health.

Some personal traits that should be encouraged by mental health professions and are vital to recovery are attitudes of purpose, faith, expectancy, and finding meaning in one's illness. Also, persons who got well had goals, options, spirituality, and role models. The belief in recovery itself is also very important in wellness, whereas the formal mental health system focuses on illness. Also, consumers/survivors do better when they don't have to relate to detached professions or a different professional every time they seek help. Consumers/survivors do better when they can relate to someone who cares about them. This is where peer counseling and consumer groups can help as well.

The National Research Project says that the mental health system needs to have a new paradigm based on the following:

1. Mental health services should be recovery enhancing respecting the patient's life experience and expertise.

2. People should be empowered by gaining control over their lives and involved in the consumer movement

3. Holistic treatment in which a person is seen as more than a disease should be implemented

4. There should be an emphasis on hope, positive mental health, and wellness instead of just biochemical imbalances and medication.

While the hospital and formal mental health care system provide the expertise on medication, it is largely up to the individual patient to work on getting well. Social connectedness, and feeling part of a community are key components in recovery and left to the individual to work on. Finding role models is important as well. In the United States there are safe houses where a person in crisis can talk to peer counselors. I would like to see the day when that happens in Canada. It would be ideal to build a center where the mentally ill could get both medical advice and also be able to talk to other consumer/survivors who could give us hope and encouragement.

7.
IS REALITY THERAPY IN REALITY?

William Glasser who wrote the book, Reality Therapy, became a psychologist in 1947 and a psychiatrist in 1957 in the days when Freud was in fashion and mental illness was explained by unconscious conflicts. Today, mental illness is considered to be a biochemical imbalance in the brain. In an address at The Evolution of Psychotherapy Conference on Sunday May, 2000 Glasser commented, " ... Regardless of the cause, psychological or chemical, the belief that mental illness is real and those suffering from it have little or no control over their symptoms has yet to be seriously challenged." He throws down the gauntlet by contending that there is no such thing as mental illness, that there are just unhappy people who have made the wrong choices.

Glasser asserts, "I contend that when we are unable to figure out how to satisfy one or more of our five basic needs built into our genetic structure that are the source of all human motivation, we sometimes choose to behave in ways that are currently labeled mental illness. These needs, explained in detail in Choice Theory, are: survival, love and belonging, power, freedom and fun. What is common to these ineffective and unsatisfying choices, no matter what they may be, is unhappiness: there is no happiness in the DSM-IV... the choice to be unhappy is not mental illness."

In his address at Anaheim, California, Glasser bolsters his opinion by citing Thomas Szaz and Peter Breggin as psychiatric experts who he has a high regard for. Glasser cites Breggin as one of the world's leading experts on brain drugs. According to the former, "Many of them (brain drugs) actually harm the brain and render it unable to function normally. For example, the drug makes it harder for many patients to figure out how to satisfy their needs as well as they would be able to do without the drug. By applying Reality Therapy, Glasser claims to have helped seriously symptomatic patients to function normally without the use of drugs.

The reason we are exploring Reality Therapy is that many of the mentally ill will meet a reality therapist during the course of their treatment. I think that Reality Therapy has become popular as a "fix it yourself" therapy that fits into a mental health care system that has suffered cut backs and patient overloads. Also, after a brief training period the reality therapist comes back sounding sagacious and authoritative. Gone is empathy because if the patient is miserable he or she is promptly told to make different choices or judgmentally blamed for being the one responsible. It's just another case of blame the victim. When in a deep depression I certainly resented being told that I was miserable because it was all my fault. I felt angry and assaulted. I also will not throw my medication into the river, because it has helped me lead a more normal life.

Many mental health consumers are sick and poor and this grossly limits the choices they can make. Being unable to work, they cannot choose their income, and often are stuck in substandard housing. Often they have lost out on a good social life and are struggling with unbearable pain. To the rich and healthy the number of nice choices increases. Maybe reality therapy works best for the well to do who can move where they want to, have a great career, enjoy lots of friendships and feel vibrant health.

Another thing about Reality Therapy that I don't buy is that it advocates a "create your own reality" kind of thing. Life does nasty things to people and sometimes one is caught between the devil and the deep blue sea. What if all my choices involve me in equal misery? Am I then supposed to rejoice because I have made a different choice? Am I supposed to delude myself into feeling happy if I am broke, sick, and lonely?

In my opinion William Glasser is going against science when he says that mental illness does not exist. Scientists are finding that low serotonin causes certain kinds of depression and illnesses like schizophrenia have been linked to too much dopamine in the brain. What makes Glasser think that the brain cannot get sick? Every other part of the body is subject to illness. Genetic markers are being found for manic depression and many other mental disorders.

On the positive side of Reality Therapy some people do need to make better choices in their life and have gotten into problems of their own making. Probably, we all need to make better choices. However, there is no call to insult a schizophrenic or bipolar person by telling them that all their misery is their own fault.

8.
WHAT IS W.R.A.P.?

When I attended the National Symposium on Empowerment in Montreal last year, I was introduced to the WRAP program by activist Carol Hayes Collier who haled from New York. WRAP stands for Wellness Recovery Action Plan and it was developed by Mary Ellen Copeland, a psychiatric survivor herself. It's purpose is to empower the psychiatric survivor and reduce the need for coercion used by the mental health care system. The five foundations of WRAP are hope, personal responsibility, education, self-advocacy, and developing and maintaining a support system. The wellness tools that WRAP encourages are thoughts and behaviors that maximize wellness and minimize symptoms, reaching out for support, peer counseling, planning the day, stress reduction, dialog with health care providers, diversionary activities, journaling, and having fun to reduce stress.

The WRAP program includes a five section plan starting with daily maintenance, indicating triggers, or early warning signs of illness, a plan for when things are breaking down, and finally a crisis strategy.

I filled out an Advanced Health Care Directive, taking the form out of Mary Ellen Copeland's book. She writes, "Some people relieve worry about possible or short term health emergencies by developing, "Advance Directives" that give supporters directions on how they want to be treated and cared for in the event that they lose the ability to make these decisions for themselves. I have had recurring episodes of severe, suicidal depression in the past. When I was well I realized that, by not having an emergency plan for my supporters, I was putting my health and life at risk. Although it was hard to think of the possibility of experiencing such deep despair again, I felt it was in my best interest and in the interest of my family and friends to develop for them a set of instructions to use as a guide in case I got very depressed again. It has helped me control worry for everyone involved."

The Advance Directive lists what circumstances or symptoms indicate when others may need to take over for you and includes the names and phone numbers of these persons. It also includes the name or names of persons who you do not want involved in your care. What medications you are on are listed as well as medications that you would prefer to avoid are mentioned. Likewise what treatments you would consent to and what treatments you would refuse are included as are the names of treatment facilities you would like to be handled in and those you would not want. Finally, there is a listing of what you need to be done and who you would want to do it when you are incapacitated.

The WRAP program gives the psychiatric survivor increased awareness of his or her illness and develops specific plans to implement when acute illness strikes.

Survivors are too often coerced and this plan gives us more control over our treatment. On the Internet there is a four week Mental Health Recovery Correspondence Course featuring WRAP that is open to anyone who wants to increase their understanding of mental health recovery. The site is found at http://www/mentalhealthrecovery.com/course/index.html . The cost is $200 American dollars plus texts, but I think that it would be well worthwhile.

9.
SHOULD I GO SEE THE PSYCHIATRIST WELL DRESSED?

What is mental illness and what does it look like? The National Alliance for the Mentally Ill (NAMI) says that, "Mental illnesses are disorders of the brain that disrupt a person's thinking, feeling, moods, and the ability to relate to others. Just as diabetes is a disorder of the pancreas, mental illnesses are brain disorders that often result in a diminished capacity for coping with the ordinary demands of life." Who gets mental illness? NAMI reports, "Mental illnesses can affect persons of any age, race, religion, or income. Mental illnesses are not the result of personal weakness, lack of character, or poor upbringing." While some therapists like Peter Breggin, and William Glasser deny this medical model, saying that mental illness does not exist, they are in the minority as science finds genes for bipolar illness and physical abnormalities in the brain that cause schizophrenia.

When asked what mental illness is, therapist, Mike Sonier commented, "I see mental illness separately from people who struggle emotionally. I think that if you look at mental illness very narrowly mental illness would be something that is physically due to a bio-chemical imbalance and inability to respond to your environment. ... Then you cross over into people who struggle emotionally and psychologically due to life experiences. I don't necessarily perceive that as mental illness ... People may as a result of having experienced a very traumatic thing may develop a way of perceiving and responding to their environment in ways that may be out of the ordinary." Conversely, Sonier continues, " Mental health is not the absence of struggle. It not the absence of thoughts that one might wonder about, it is how well one struggles with those thoughts ... If one is not struggling well, then it leaves you with anxiety, depression, those types of things which keep you from where you want to be in life."

If mental illness is no respecter of persons, do therapists or even the patients they treat have certain mis-perceptions of what a mentally ill person is supposed to look like? Could they identity a mentally ill person from a non-mentally ill person on the street? The interviews that were conducted included two therapists and three clients. All said that mentally ill people looked like everybody else. One therapist said that the medication side effects identified certain body postures that identified the ill person. He also mentioned that some of the mentally ill walk with their heads down.

Another question that was asked in the interviews was, Does it make a difference in the therapist's assessment of the patient's mental state if the latter is poorly dressed or poorly groomed? or conversely well dressed and well groomed? Mike Sonier, commented that, " If a client has had a history of not keeping themselves and I have learned to interpret that as being an indication of how well they're doing, it could be that how they present themselves could be an indication of how well they're doing psychologically. ... A depressed person for instance. It will show in their demeanor and the way they keep themselves. When a person is doing well inwardly, it tends to show outwardly, but just because the outward is O.K that doesn't mean that that's a reflection of what's happening inside. I'll certainly take the outward appearance into consideration, but I will go with what he/she is saying."

When a client, L.S., was interviewed she commented, "If I'm well dressed and well groomed. They (the therapists) think that great improvement have occurred. If I'm not so well dressed and not so well groomed they think that I'm not taking care of myself and my mental illness is taking over my life. Commenting on being well dressed, L.S. said, "... it just means I'm wearing something different. Not getting better at all it just means that that day I'm just dressed a different way." D.G., also a client, disagreed with this and felt that his appearance did not make a difference to the therapist. However, R. F. the third client said that because he decided to grow a beard, he was told by a professional that he was, "Letting himself go." Perhaps some therapists have underlying mis-perceptions of the clients that need to be challenged. Just because the client comes to the therapy session looking well groomed on the outside, doesn't mean that he/she is not in mental anguish. In conclusion, if you the client are a lot of psychological pain, don't go to the therapist's office looking too good, or you might get a slap on the back and told, "You're doing just fine!" Mental illness can be an invisible disease, with all the hurting festering inside.

D. POEMS ON EXPERIENCING MENTAL ILLNESS

KATHERINE TAPLEY-MILTON

MIND FULL OF SCORPIONS

Bad memories
sting the mind
like scorpions ...
their venom
biting deep
into consciousness;
wounding, scarring,
violating tender tissues,
even time the alleged healer,
cannot erase
the pain.

KATHERINE TAPLEY-MILTON

ANOTHER COLD MORNING

Longing
for a human touch
like a starving man's
passion for food:
aching for intimacy
but waking up alone;
hoping for tenderness,
but finding
only another
cold morning.

NO CRY FOR HELP

Festering wounds
Of a thousand different traumas
Bubble and boil to the surface
And the conscious mind collapses
Like mud huts swept away under
A volcanic eruption of lava.
Evening falls
Like a smothering blanket
Of despair,
Suffocating the brightness
And openness of the daylight
Into lurking shadows
Of sin, despair, and doom.
Depression feeds
Under its dark cloak
And eats like an acid
Into the soul.
There is no strength left
Even to cry for help.

KATHERINE TAPLEY-MILTON

WHEN FEELINGS HOWL

On this useless night
of continual soul aching,
I wonder why life turns brutal.
My feelings in daylight hours
stay locked in safety deposit boxes,
But when the sparkling sun
dips down on the blood red horizon
my emotions howl like a furious blizzard.
Fear, anger, love, guilt, rage
all whip my psyche to battered bits.
Scenes of the past
flash like a kaleidoscope
of Stephen King movies;
until I fall exhausted into a psychotropic sleep.

MAD HISTORY LESSON

By
Katherine Tapley-Milton

Remember the psychiatrized
In chains and open sewers,
Rats gnawing at their flesh.
Hidden away in attics,
Crying and moaning in institutions.
The first to be sent to gas chambers
By Hitler;
Plunged into ice baths,
Electroshocked, lobotomized, dehumanized.
Forsaken by kin,
Shunned by polite society.
Rejected, and shamed.
Condemned to grinding poverty.
Let's have a moment of silence,
Then speak with one voice
That the atrocities must end.

KATHERINE TAPLEY-MILTON

MAD WOMAN WALKING

Disguised as normal
I walk the streets
As a madwoman.
Always faking it,
For God, for others, for society
Seldom acting on
Mad thoughts and impulses.
Walking circumspectly,
Avoiding the cops
Who can drag you off to a hospital
Where they can legally fry
Your brains to death.
Denied life insurance
Because I'm "depressed",
Coping with madness,
Which is scorned and mocked
In nearly every conversation. I hear.
When I never saying my true feelings,
I fit in.
But, at times the madness
Overflows and leaks out
All over the sidewalk,
And splatters shocked people
Who judge and shame me.

THE TIME-WORN MAIDEN

"Save me!" cries the distressed damsel
to her knight in rusty armour.
"Save me from the winter night
which has most cruelly descended,
and the cold that is freezing my bones.
Deliver me from those ravening wolves
Who seek to rend my sanity apart.
Save me from the hypocrites
Who pose as martyrs
And smile false smiles.
Stay with me when my soul has been
Crushed by my own kin
And bleeds.
Wipe away all the silent tears
Of anguish and outrage
That fall upon
My fevered brow.
Lie down with me
And sooth me with
Your sweet nectar kisses
And tender caresses.
For this world
Has proved to be
No friend of mine.

KATHERINE TAPLEY-MILTON

THE CRUCIFYING PLACE

By
Katherine Tapley-Milton

Muscles protesting in surging agony
My body to world-weary to move
And the committee
In my head
Screaming, keening
That I must die today.
There is no strength
To cry out anymore,
After forty years in the wilderness,
It feels like
No one cares for my soul.
So I've come to the
Crucifying place,
The silent, shameful, haemorrhaging
Of the mind
Located in the Valley of dry bones
Where egg white, brittle skeletons rattle loud
Enough to wake the dead;
An apex of agony
When even God
Seems to have left
The receiver off the hook,
And all there is left
Are silent, inner screams
For a Rapture or an ending.

THE WAITING ROOMS OF LIFE

I am the foetus, waiting nine months to be born
Then I am the baby, from the womb I am torn.
Next I am the ankle nipper waiting to talk
Then I am the yard ape waiting to walk.
Adolescence comes and my hormones are raging
I wait for a lover—in carnal knowledge
I am engaging.
A long search goes on for a mate
to my very lonely soul
Someone whom I could live with,
some person to make me whole.
I wait and I wait for my mate to appear
And one day I find him on the Internet so near.
I wait for engagement and I wait for marriage
Then I wait for a baby to put into our carriage.
I have problems with my marriage
and problems with my kids
My life as I know it is really on the skids.
Now I wait for the psychiatrist
who is going to read my head
And I take all colours of pills
that are supposed to fix my head.
Midlife hits us and I am wondering
what I've done with my life
And I see that most of my existence
has been bitterness and strife,
Now I am a cynical old person waiting to die
Put into a nursing home
so others can pass me by.
I wait for the doctor, I wait for the nurse,
Now I am waiting for the man
who drives the hearse.

KATHERINE TAPLEY-MILTON

The funeral is over and my body is laid to rest
The waiting rooms of life are over
and so is my quest.
To heaven or hell I'll be immediately ushered in
God will weigh every thought and every single sin.
I'll either be found wanting or finally be approved.
But my eternal state will never be moved.

ZOMBIE

By
Katherine Tapley-Milton

Walking in a waking dream
Dreaming I'm awake,
People and cars moving
In slow motion
Numbness and unreality
Merge with world-weariness
Maybe somebody
Threw zombie powder
On me without my knowledge
So I'm neither alive
Nor dead
Cursed to wander
The earth
Looking for a grave;
Dead woman walking.

KATHERINE TAPLEY-MILTON

DAYS OF BLOOD AND CHOCOLATE

I hide my madness in my
Kitchen cupboard
And it comes out
Like a horrendous looking troll
When it chooses to.
The chocolate
from the cake I baked
Drips down my arm
And for a moment
I mistake it for blood.
So much blood has
Flowed from jagged
Razor cuts
And yet the shame
Continues on.
I have enough shame
To supply the entire world.
Silent scars give their
Testimony to stunned onlookers
Who have no idea of
The miniature Medieval
Torture chamber
Inside my cranium
The chocolate and the blood
It's all mixed together now
Who knows what's normal?

WHEN THE CURTAIN DESCENDED

I was once a small, innocent girl
Watering the geraniums
In my grandmother's greenhouse
Happy in innocence,
Elfin, blissful.
But puberty came and
The dark curtain
Descended;
And brought the minions
Of Nazi death soldiers who
March in my head,
Cracking reality,
Shooting holes in my innocence,
Their voices constantly barking;
Commanding my demise.
But though the curtain descended
The play goes on with no exit
Now, I am a war- weary knight
Of the night time
Who has taken too many sword wounds
To the heart.
Bitter experience shatters my innocence,
Dark depression blots out the bliss,
And I keep wondering
What went wrong
In heaven or on earth,
That made even the Almighty
Forsake me.

E. SAMPLE LEGAL FORMS

Please check with a lawyer to see what forms are legal in your province or state. These forms are examples only.

Power Of Attorney For Personal Care

PERSONAL CARE:
I (full name) (full address)

of

Appoint the following person(s) to be my attorney(s) for personal care to act jointly or severally. (full name and address of all appointed attorneys to be inserted on the following lines)

I authorize my attorney(s), on my behalf, to make any personal care decisions for me that I am incapable of making for myself, including the giving or refusing of consent to medical treatment.
I do /I do not want you to use life support systems or to take extreme measures to prolong my life if there is no reasonable possible hope of my recovery. In those circumstances, please allow me to die a natural death with a minimum of pain and anxiety.
(please circle your preference for this paragraph)
Date:

(signature)

Witnesses

ADVANCE DIRECTIVE FOR MENTAL HEALTH TREATMENT

Some people relieve worry about possible short or long term health emergencies by developing advanced health directives that give supporters directions on how they want to be treated and cared for in the event that they lose the ability to make these decisions for themselves.

I have had recurring episodes of severe, suicidal depression in the past. When I was well I realized that, by not having an emergency plan for my supporters, I was putting my health and life at risk. Although it was hard to think of the possibility of experiencing such deep despair again, I felt it was in my best interest and the best interest of my family and friends to develop for them a set of instructions to use as a guide in case I got very depressed again. It has helped control worry for everyone involved."

Mary Ellen Copeland

The following information was obtained from the "Duke University Program on Psychiatric Advanced Directives" http:pad.duhs.duke.edu/ . It seems that many provinces in Canada do not have this protective legislation. I think that it is something that we should be pushing our legislators for.

In many provinces advanced directives are not legally binding, but may have some influence in treatment.

KATHERINE TAPLEY-MILTON

(Please refer to the Psychiatric Advance Directives Toolkit for instructions to complete this worksheet.)

1. Symptom(s) I might experience during a period of crisis:

2. Medication instructions.
a. I agree to administration of the following medication(s):

b. I do not agree to administration of the following medication(s):

c. Other information about medications (allergies, side effects)

3. Facility Preferences.
a. I agree to admission to the following hospital(s):

b. I do not agree to admission to the following hospital(s):

c. Other information about hospitalization:

4. Emergency Contacts in case of mental health crisis:
Name:
Address:

Home Phone #
Work Phone#
Relationship to Me:

Name:
Address:

Home Phone #
Work Phone#
Relationship to Me:

Psychiatrist:
Work Phone#

Case Manager/Therapist:
Work Phone #

5. Crisis Precipitants. The following may cause me to experience a mental health crisis:

6. Protective Factors. The following may help me avoid a mental health crisis:

7. Response to Hospital. I usually respond to the hospital as follows:

8. Preferences for Staff Interactions.
a. Staff of the hospital or crisis unit can help me by doing the following:

b. Staff can minimize use of restraint and seclusion by doing the following:

9. I give permission for the following people to visit me in the hospital:

10. The following are my preferences about ECT:

11. Other Instructions.
a. If I am hospitalized, I want the following to be taken care of at my home:

b. I understand that the information in this document may be shared by my mental health treatment provider with any other mental health treatment provider who may serve me when necessary to provide treatment in accordance with this advance instruction. Other instructions about sharing of information are as follows:

12. Legal documentation for Advance Directives:

Signature of Principal

By signing here, I indicate that I am mentally alert and competent, fully informed as to the contents of this document, and understand the full impact of having made this advance instruction for mental health treatment.

Signature of Principal

Date

Nature of Witnesses

I hereby state that the principal is personally known to me, that the principal signed or acknowledged the principal's signature on this advance instruction for mental health treatment in my presence, that the principal appears to be of sound mind and not under duress, fraud, or undue influence, and that I am not:

The attending physician or mental health service provider or an employee of the physician or mental health treatment provider;

An owner, operator, or employee of an owner or operator of a health care facility in which the principal is a patient or resident; or

Related within the third degree to the principal or to the principal's spouse.

Affirmation of Witnesses

We affirm that the principal is personally known to us, that the principal signed or acknowledged the principal's signature on this advance instruction for mental health treatment in our presence, that the principal appears to be of sound mind and not under duress, fraud, or undue influence, and that neither of us is: A person appointed as an attorney-in-fact by this document; The principal's attending physician or mental health service provider or a relative of the physician or provider; The owner, operator, or relative of an owner or operator of a facility in which the principal is a patient or resident; or A person related to the principal by blood, marriage, or adoption.

Witnessed by:

Witness:

Date:

Witness:

Date:

STATE OF NORTH CAROLINA, COUNTY OF

Certification of Notary Public

STATE OF NORTH CAROLINA COUNTY OF

I, _____ , a Notary Public for the County cited above in the State of North Carolina, hereby certify that _____ appeared before me and swore or affirmed to me and to the witnesses in my presence that this instrument is an advance instruction for mental health treatment, and that he/she willingly and voluntarily made and executed it as his/her free act and deed for the purposes expressed in it.

I further certify that _____ and _____ , witnesses, appeared before me and swore or affirmed that they witnessed _____ sign the attached advance instruction for mental health treatment, believing him/her to be of sound mind; and also swore that at the time they witnessed the signing they were not (i) the attending physician or mental health treatment provider or an employee of the physician or mental health treatment provider and (ii) they were not an owner, operator, or employee of an owner or operator of a health care facility in which the principal is a patient or resident, and (iii) they were not related within the third degree to the principal or to the principal's spouse. I further certify that I am satisfied as to the genuineness and due execution of the instrument.

    This is the _____ day of _____, 20___.

    Notary Public
    My Commission expires:

Statutory Notices

Notice to Person Making an Instruction For Mental Health Treatment. This is an important legal document. It creates an instruction for mental health treatment. Before signing this document you should know these important facts: This document allows you to make decisions in advance about certain types of mental health treatment. The instructions you include in this declaration will be followed if a physician or eligible psychologist determines that you are incapable of making and communicating treatment decisions. Otherwise you will be considered capable to give or withhold consent for the treatments. Your instructions may be overridden if you are being held in accordance with civil commitment law. Under the Health Care Power of Attorney you may also appoint a person as your health care agent to make treatment decisions for you if you become incapable. You have the right to revoke this document at any time you have not been determined to be incapable. YOU MAY NOT REVOKE THIS ADVANCE INSTRUCTION WHEN YOU ARE FOUND INCAPABLE BY A PHYSICIAN OR OTHER

AUTHORIZED MENTAL HEALTH TREATMENT PROVIDER. A revocation is effective when it is communicated to your attending physician or other provider. The physician or other provider shall note the revocation in your medical record. To be valid, this advance instruction must be signed by two qualified witnesses, personally known to you, who are present when you sign or acknowledge your signature. It must also be acknowledged before a notary public.

Notice to Physician or Other Mental Health Treatment Provider. Under North Carolina law, a person may use this advance instruction to provide consent for future mental health treatment if the person later becomes incapable of making those decisions. Under the Health Care Power of Attorney the person may also appoint a health care agent to make mental health treatment decisions for the person when incapable. A person is "incapable" when in the opinion of a physician or eligible psychologist the person currently lacks sufficient understanding or capacity to make and communicate mental health treatment decisions. This document becomes effective upon its proper execution and remains valid unless revoked. Upon being presented with this advance instruction, the physician or other provider must make it a part of the person's medical record. The attending physician or other mental health treatment provider must act in accordance with the statements expressed in the advance instruction when the person is determined to be incapable, unless compliance is not consistent with G.S. 122C-74(g). The physician or other mental health treatment provider shall promptly notify the principal and, if applicable, the health care agent, and document noncompliance with any part of an advance instruction in the principal's medical record. The physician or other mental health treatment provider may rely upon the authority of a signed, witnessed, dated, and notarized advance instruction, as provided in G.S. 122C-75. (1997-442, s. 2; 1998-198, s. 2; 1998-217, s. 53(a)(5).)

PSYCHIATRIC ADVANCE DIRECTIVE TOOLKIT

Drafting a Psychiatric Advance Directive.

North Carolina has a way you can plan ahead for mental health treatment you might want to receive if you are in a crisis and are unable to communicate for yourself or make voluntary decisions of your own free will. An Advance Directive for Mental Health Treatment allows you to write down treatment preferences or instructions if you had a crisis in the future and could not make your own mental health treatment decisions. This toolkit will walk you through filling out an Advance Directive for Mental Health Treatment document in twelve quick steps.

What are Psychiatric Advance Directives?

On an Advance Directives Document, people can describe the kind of mental health treatment they want to receive if they cannot make decisions for themselves in the future. This can include a person's wishes about medications, ECT, or admission to a hospital. It is important to realize that someone can change these forms at any time if they wish.

How might Psychiatric Advance Directives be of benefit?

One benefit is that people can document what medications they would want or not want in a crisis. Another benefit is that people can say what hospital they would want or not want to be admitted to in a crisis. Psychiatric advance directives, or PADs, can tell clinical staff how people would want to be treated while in the hospital (like being treated with respect). They can also tell clinical staff their personal preferences (not to be bound, etc.) for treatment. Finally, people can choose someone they trust (like a family member) to make treatment decisions for them if they cannot make the decisions themselves.

What are limitations of Psychiatric Advance Directives?

It is important to realize when these forms are used; people may have changed their minds about the treatment they want. Also, their chosen person may not do exactly what they have asked them to do in the PAD. It is also the case that the hospitals people wish to be admitted to may not have beds at the time of a crisis. Finally, doctors can still use involuntary commitment and do not have to provide treatment they believe is inappropriate.

When are Psychiatric Advance Directives especially important?

One especially important use of advance directives is that you may choose to give instructions in advance of a crisis to people taking care of you during a crisis. For example, you may decide that in a crisis you would like a trusted person to make any important decisions for you based on what they think is the right decision. You could also put in an advance instruction "please call my doctor or clinician and follow his/her instructions". That way, if you are in an emergency room or in a clinic, if you are unable to speak for yourself or very confused, these instructions can be used as a means to try to help you at vital moments.

How can Psychiatric Advance Directives be filled out?

If you are interested in completing an Advance Directives Document, please print out a blank copy of the Advance Directives for Mental Health Treatment worksheet and walk through the following easy steps:

Step 1. Crisis Symptoms.

The first thing you may choose to write in the Advance Directives document is the kind of symptoms you have when you get into a crisis. These symptoms would include mental or physical signs indicating your mental health is getting worse. Listing these symptoms could help treatment providers recognize early warning signs you may be experiencing problems. The more specific you can be, the more information you communicate to future providers about the condition.

Step 2. Medications.

Next you can describe preferences for medications. If you wish, answer any of the following:

Are there any particular psychiatric medications that you would like to request in a crisis? Which ones?

Are there any medications you do not want to receive in a crisis? If so, which ones? Why?

Are there any medications that you are allergic to or you have had bad reactions to? If so, what are the medications you are allergic to?

Step 3. Facility Preferences.

You can also describe preferences for hospitals. If you wish, answer any of the following:

Are there specific hospitals you would prefer to go to in the future? Why?

Are there hospitals you would prefer not to go to in the future? Why?

Do you want to leave this decision to your health care agent? If so, please write this request.

Step 4. Emergency Contacts.

Here, you can list the names, addresses, and phone numbers of people you would want contacted in an emergency. You can also include information about your physician/psychiatrist or case manager/therapist.

Step 5. Crisis Precipitants.

It may be helpful to write down the sort of things that cause you to experience a mental health crisis. If you cannot think of anything, you can list certain situations that are particularly stressful to you.

Step 6. Protective Factors.

It may also be helpful to list things that can help you avoid a hospitalization. Are there things that you feel would save you from having an unwanted hospitalization?

Step 7. Usual Response to Hospital.

You have the opportunity to write down how you react to a hospitalization. Thinking back on your hospitalizations, are there specific ways you react? Do certain aspects of being in the hospital make you feel uncomfortable? If so, you can list these here.

Step 8. Preferences for Staff Interactions.

1. It would be helpful to let the hospital or crisis unit know what they may do to help you in a crisis. Are there specific things staff can do for you to make you more comfortable or relaxed?
2. It would be helpful to provide instructions in advance for staff to intervene if you were feeling out of control. What things would help to minimize chances of being restrained and/or secluded?

Step 9. Visitation Permission.

You may give permission here for people to visit you in the hospital.

Step 10. ECT Preferences.

Electro-Convulsive Therapy (ECT), sometimes referred in the past as shock therapy, is a type of treatment that is occasionally used in severe episodes of mental illness, primarily depression. Typically, it is used after multiple trials of medications have failed, but may also be used earlier when a rapid response is urgently needed and/or the patient requests. Here, you can write your preferences for ECT. If you don't have a preference, you can write that you want your doctor to decide for you in the future regarding the need for ECT. You can also ask that your Health Care Agent to be informed before ECT treatment is administered.

Step 11. Other Instructions.

You can list any other instructions you want. Some examples are writing instructions about paying rent or feeding pets while you are in the hospital and listing any other medical conditions you want doctors to be aware of.

In this next part, you are being told that advance directives can be shared with others on your treatment team if necessary. If you have any specific instructions regarding sharing of this information, list it here.

Step 12. Legal Documentation.

As principal, you should read through the entire document to ensure it is accurate. You must have some identification I.D. to show the notary.

Witnesses cannot be family members or anyone working at the mental health center; neighbors or friends are okay but they too must have I.D..

The notary fills out this section and stamps the document.

These two notices are from the North Carolina statute and need to be included on your Advance Directive for Mental Health Treatment.

F. HELPFUL WEBSITES

www.ourvoice-notrevoix.com This website contains past issues of a consumer/survivor articles and poems and is published by editor Eugene Leblanc at P.O. Box 29004, Moncton, NB, Canada., E1G 4R3. Our Voice/Notre Voix has a circulation that goes to a significant number of foreign countries, as well as having a Canadian circulation. Just about every consumer/survivor issue is contained in this magazine and it is all consumer/survivor written.

www.MindFreedom.org is a website managed by David Oaks from Eugene, Oregon who is an anti-electroshock activist. His motto is "Win human rights in the mental health system."

www.selfhelpconnection.ca is a website that is a clearinghouse for mental health information and support in Atlantic Canada.

www.nami.org is an American website that provides information on mental illness, medication, etc. . It also does mental health advocacy.

www.prozactruth.com/ has some interesting information on coping with the weight gain that comes as a side effect of certain psychiatric medications. It also has some advice about getting off medications more comfortably.

www.mooddisorders.on.ca is an organization devoted to educating the public and consumer/survivors about bipolar illness.

www.cmha.ca is the Canadian Mental Health Association's main website that offers educational material on mental illness and ways to cope with it. On the site there is a map of all the local branches that are in each province.